Praise for Triss Stein

BROOKLYN WARS
The Fourth Erica Donato Mystery

"Triss Stein's Erica Donato series contains my favorite brew of mystery ingredients: a strong sense of place, history, and character. Brooklyn, the symbol of all things both modern and retro, again anchors this fourth installment. As historian Erica investigates another murder, the former heyday of the Brooklyn Navy Yard will be revisited, proving that the past never really dies."

—Naomi Hirahara, Edgar Award-winning author of *Hiroshima Boy*

"A mother, a daughter, a dead body. Family lore, politics, and history combine in a high-stakes story as historian Erica Donato investigates murder, Brooklyn-style. In *Brooklyn Wars*, Triss Stein again brings her slice of New York, past and present, to vivid life."

—James R. Benn, author of the Billy Boyle World War II Mystery series

"Readers who enjoyed Clea Simon's 'Dulcie Schwartz' mysteries for the doctoral student aspects, or Mary Anna Evans's books involving history, might enjoy this series."

—*Library Journal*

"Stein's sure hand weaves history and mystery together for a colorful tale of love, loss, greed, and murder."

—*Publishers Weekly*

BROOKLYN SECRETS

The Third Erica Donato Mystery

"A gripping page-turner... Suspenseful and engaging."
—Annamaria Alfieri, author of *Strange Gods*

"Brooklyn's rich history comes to life in Stein's wonderful descriptions, and Erica is an engaging tour guide."

—*Booklist*

BROOKLYN GRAVES

The Second Erica Donato Mystery

"Even more absorbing than the well-plotted mystery is her vibrant depiction of Brooklyn."
—Margaret Maron, *New York Times* bestselling author

"Stein's second issues-oriented series entry is an enticing introduction to Brooklyn's immigrant history. This perfect tie-in with Susan Vreeland's historical novel, *Clara and Mr. Tiffany,* will also appeal to Kathleen Ernst and Joan Hess (Claire Malloy series) readers."

—*Library Journal*

"The independent Erica is an interesting character, too, especially for her era: a widow earning her PhD in history while working part-time who has difficult relationships with her teenage daughter and her somewhat overbearing father. A couple of possible love interests on the horizon add to the appeal of this engaging historical-mystery series."

—*Booklist*

"Stein gives an economical but vivid sense of Erica's Brooklyn neighborhood, and the characterization is wonderful—especially the wryly self-aware narrator's recognition of how much her own confusion is mirrored in her daughter's behavior."

—*Publishers Weekly*

BROOKLYN BONES

The First Erica Donato Mystery

"A delicious, classic mystery."

—Michele Martinez, author of the Melanie Vargas Mysteries

"Family ties lie at the heart of this book, and the way they are woven into the mystery will be sure to surprise."

—*Library Journal*

BROOKLYN LEGACIES

Also by Triss Stein

The Erica Donato Mysteries

Brooklyn Bones

Brooklyn Graves

Brooklyn Secrets

Brooklyn Wars

BROOKLYN LEGACIES

AN ERICA DONATO MYSTERY

TRISS STEIN

The characters and events portrayed in this book are fictitious or are used fictitiously. Any similarity to real persons, living or dead, is purely coincidental and not intended by the author.

Published by Poisoned Pen Press, an imprint of Sourcebooks
P.O. Box 4410, Naperville, Illinois 60567-4410
(630) 961-3900
sourcebooks.com

Library of Congress Cataloging-in-Publication Data

Names: Stein, Triss, author.
Title: Brooklyn legacies / Triss Stein.
Description: Naperville, Illinois : Poisoned Pen Press, an imprint of Sourcebooks, [2019]
Identifiers: LCCN 2019027072 | (trade paperback)
Classification: LCC PS3569.T37543 B765 2019 | DDC 813/.54--dc23
LC record available at https://lccn.loc.gov/2019027072

Printed and bound in the United States of America.
SB 10 9 8 7 6 5 4 3 2 1

ACKNOWLEDGMENTS

Brooklyn Legacies is a book that needed a lot of background information. Any mistakes are all my own.

Tremendous thanks to:

Martin Schneider, who was active in the creation of the Brooklyn Heights Historic District and wrote the book. Literally. It's called *Battling for Brooklyn Heights: The Fight for New York's First Historic District*. He kindly shared many memories, answered questions and brought me the story of the Walt Whitman plaque.

Peter Bray of the Brooklyn Heights Association, who helped me connect with Martin and got me started on this story.

Sheila Lowe, author of the Forensic Handwriting Mysteries series, who repeatedly provided reality checks on that topic and also, with great generosity, shared her past as a Jehovah's Witness.

Bernard Whalen and Marco Conelli, fellow members of Mystery Writers of America–New York Chapter. By cheerfully sharing information from their years in law enforcement, they save us all from silly mistakes.

Thomas Dunne, retired deputy chief and thirty-three-year-veteran of the New York City Fire Department, who answered many questions about what actually happens at, and after, a fire. More saving from silly mistakes.

As always, the extremely helpful and expert staff at the Brooklyn Public Library's Brooklyn Collection and their invaluable files.

Queens Mystery Writers Group. We talk, we eat, we support each other, we figure it out. Laura Joh Rowland, Nancy Bilyeau, Jen Kitses, Mariah Frederick, Shizuka Otake, and Radha Vatsal.

And my family, as always.

Chapter One

When I was growing up in Brooklyn, I didn't even know a place like Brooklyn Heights existed. In my neighborhood, people didn't see much reason to leave home. An excursion to Manhattan once a year was considered plenty. On the way, I could see Brooklyn Heights as we crossed a bridge into "the city," but I could not see much. There were the roofs of the low buildings. A sprawling complex with a gigantic mysterious sign—WATCHTOWER—on its roof dominated everything else. It looked a little ominous.

The first time I really saw the Heights was when a college professor commanded us to visit the famous Brooklyn Heights Promenade. We were studying the conflicts between neighborhood activists and city planners—not a new story and certainly not unique to Brooklyn—and the promenade was born of an important early battle over homes versus highways. He told us to find our way to Brooklyn Heights. Didn't we know a direct subway line ran right past the Brooklyn College campus?

I discovered a whole neighborhood of quaint brick row houses interspersed with later, more elaborate brownstones, scattered apartment buildings, and a couple of gigantic, once-elegant, hotels. How had I not known about this?

As I wandered away from the busy commercial district, the

streets became hushed, the houses even older. The pavement was dotted with patches of cobblestone. I had the strangest feeling that I might turn a corner and find something unexpected, even magical, a stray cat that could actually whistle up a storm, an antique shop where the owner was a magician, a mouse who had his own sailboat, a library with a book that told me how to become a wizard.

Back then I was still young enough to have childhood books still alive in my mind, although I thought I'd outgrown them all.

To my further astonishment I walked past a three-story frame house, built right out to the sidewalk, looking like a colonial house from—where?—New England? I'd never been to any other state except New Jersey, but I had seen pictures. How could this be the same Brooklyn I called home?

It didn't look like the site of the vicious civic battles our professor had described. I shook off the fantasies and started taking notes for class. The charming surface was not our assignment.

Years later I was sneaking in a short, reminiscent look around before I had a genuine work meeting. It was a beautiful bright fall day with a crisp breeze off the harbor. I was a different person by then.

I had written a dissertation chapter on those civic battles. I had worked nearby for a while at a small Brooklyn history museum. By then I was a grad student in history, a single mother of a teenager, a widow with not one minute for exploring any neighborhood. Barely enough time to sleep.

Still, it was always worth stealing a few minutes for the promenade. The broad walkway with benches was built out over the Brooklyn-Queens Expressway, effectively both hiding the highway and giving the pedestrians a spectacular view out over the majestic harbor and the dramatic skyline of lower Manhattan. The vastness of the view and the heart-stopping beauty astounded me every time.

There were sailboats, tugboats, and barges on the water, islands, a proud display of skyscrapers across the East River, and a series of magnificent bridges in both directions. All this was born because Robert Moses, the late city-planning czar, had wanted to run the expressway right through a living neighborhood, and the neighborhood had fought for its life and won.

My dissertation chapter was about the local activists, a coalition of young families who had settled in Brooklyn's posh old neighborhood, old families who already had deep roots, and urban activists who passionately believed that preserving neighborhood life was essential for any city. It was something new for a Brooklyn neighborhood. Jane Jacobs was their patron saint. The powerful and secretive Robert Moses loomed over the dispute, expecting his much different vision to win out in the end. The building developers wanted to tear it all down and build towers.

I finally found out what "Watchtower" meant. The sign marked the world headquarters of the Jehovah's Witnesses religious organization. To my surprise, the denomination was one of the biggest property owners in Brooklyn Heights.

Having finished my degree—finally!—I now had a real job at a famous art museum. Health insurance, a title, and everything. I swung between panic that I did not understand how a real job situation worked and a firm belief that I knew what I was doing.

This day I was going to see a man about a piece of art.

We were planning to bring out of storage more of our quirky collection of architectural art. The sculpture garden already had ancient-Greek-style winged horses, a bronze dying Indian on horseback, and a miniature Statue of Liberty. No kidding. They were relics of a time when commercial building owners used art to make a statement about their property's importance and their own superior taste.

Being new, I was working hard, acquainting myself with the records on everything relevant. That's how I came across the Case of the Missing Whitman Plaque. Yes, I did secretly think of it that way. Very Nancy Drew.

The folder I found contained only a tattered local newspaper clipping from 1961 describing the bronze plaque created to identify the building where *Leaves of Grass* had been printed. Whitman himself had helped set the type.

By the time the article had been published, the organization that had commissioned the plaque was long gone, the printing shop was longer gone, the location was a small luncheonette, and the building was scheduled for demolition. Middle-income housing was going up on that shabby block. Attempts were being made to purchase the plaque and house it at the museum. And that was it. My research dead-ended there.

I had an appointment with a Dr. Kingston, a local historian who might know more. He was a retired history professor and longtime manager of the historical society in Brooklyn Heights.

An elderly man, he welcomed me with a genial smile and apologized for his office, which was crammed with file cabinets and a few pieces of shabby furniture covered with piles of folders. When he made a joke about the mess, and I replied with one about how it looked just like a historian's office should, we knew immediately that we spoke the same language.

He had a decades-old letter from the Nicaraguan consulate to the owner of the luncheonette, a Nicaraguan immigrant. Another memo established that there was no clear ownership of the plaque. A photo of the actual plaque showed an elaborate piece of bronze bas-relief, a portrait of Whitman, Brooklyn's very own genius. But there was nothing to say where it had gone. Not one thing.

Before we were ready to draw the obvious conclusion, there was a sharp rap on the outer door, and, without waiting for a response, someone came in.

"Jeremy, I must talk to you. Right now." When she appeared in the doorway of his office, her face was furious and his was red.

"Now, Louisa. Louisa! You can see I have a visitor. You'll have to make an appointment."

"I will not. I certainly will not. I must talk to you about the latest outrage from that Bible-thumping snake in the grass. I'll wait in your foyer." She turned but said over her shoulder, "Don't forget I can hear every word you say."

Who was a Bible-thumping snake? And why was this very erect white-haired woman in such a fury? In her ladylike navy suit, nylons, a smart hat with a feather, and a double string of pearls, she didn't look like someone who made a habit of going into furious rages. Her appearance was emphatically old-fashioned for these casual times. Expensive, too, if the pearls were real. The purple running shoes were a startling accessory, though, as was the gold-headed cane.

Dr. Kingston looked both annoyed and resigned. He silently mouthed to me, "Do you mind?"

Mind? I was tingling with curiosity.

"Come on in, Louisa. Meet Dr. Donato, from the Brooklyn Museum. She's going to wait to finish our meeting. For which she had an appointment, by the way."

The woman walked back in briskly, ignoring her elegant cane. She ignored me, too, and leaned on the edge of the desk instead of sitting.

"He's done it again, that old hypocrite! Sent me a claim that my garden impinges on their property line. Brotherly love, my old Brooklyn ass!"

"Well, I'm not sure brotherly love in general…"

"Oh, stop it, Jeremy. I don't care what they believe, as long as God being on their side doesn't mean stealing my property. They seem to believe I am too old to fight."

He looked at her with a calm I suspected he did not feel. "You'll never be too old to fight."

"Damn straight." She fell silent.

"So what is it this time?"

"That building they have next to me. They are selling it. Did you know?"

"Everyone knows. They're moving their headquarters upstate and selling off all their properties here."

Was he talking about the Jehovah's Witnesses and their Watchtower Society?

"They took over this whole neighborhood. Or they tried."

He silently looked at her with a faint smile, and she dialed it down a notch or two.

"Oh, all right. Only part of the neighborhood. A tax-exempt conglomerate, that's what they are. But they can't have my little bit, too."

We were getting to the heart of the issue, I thought. Could I discreetly take notes? Or maybe turn on the recording function of my phone, if I remembered how?

"Now are you going to tell me what's on your mind, or continue to waste my time? And Dr. Donato's? Yours, too."

She smiled a little, but not happily. "Right. At my age, I don't have time to waste." She took a deep breath. "The buyer's surveyor claims the property line extends all the way into my garden. In other words, they own a strip of my land. Did you ever hear of anything so ridiculous?"

"And…?"

"And? Isn't it obvious? I need you to help dig up the old deeds, prove them wrong. That's all."

"Louisa, Louisa. You know I'm sympathetic but haven't we been here before? It's not my job. I'm only here part-time, and I don't even have an assistant. You're going to have to break down and hire a real-estate attorney."

"Nope. No. No. Why should I spend the money when they are in the wrong?" He tried to respond, but she cut him off. "You could talk to him."

"Their lawyer? Not a chance."

"No. Try to follow along, Jeremy. I want you to talk to your Watchtower buddy for me. Daniel Towns. He's behind all this."

I was intrigued by her, but I was having a lot of trouble following her scattered tale of woe.

"A long way from being my buddy. We've merely worked

together cordially over the years. You know very well they've done a first-class job of restoring some of their buildings."

"Cordial? You mean unlike my dealings with him?"

He made a protesting gesture, but she went right on. "Come on. You know that was what you were thinking." She stood up at last, looking the tiniest bit less furious. "Well, that's what I came to say. Talk to him for me. Get him to see reason. You will, won't you? I need to get this done. It's my home, and my last preservation project, I expect."

She shook his hand with old-fashioned courtesy—not that she'd shown any until then—and left.

I was exploding with questions, but Dr. Kingston held up his hand.

"Give me a minute. I need a little recovery time after a visit from the grand duchess." He saw my face, shook his head, and gulped the last of his coffee from a paper cup. "No, she's not really a duchess, though she might have some delusions in that direction. She is Louisa McWilliams Gibbs, who is certainly the duchess of Brooklyn Heights."

"Seriously?" I squeaked. "*The* Louisa Gibbs? I didn't know she was still…I mean, I thought…"

"Oh, yes, she is still around. That's what you're not saying, isn't it? Alive and kicking and still able to be a serious pain in the patoot for the local history community."

"I read her books in at least two classes. She is a giant. I wish I had known. I would have said something. She was…she is…"

He smiled at my incoherent fan-girl reaction, and I was embarrassed. What am I, a teenager meeting a rock star? Actually, my real teen daughter would be cooler than me. A humiliating thought.

But Louisa Gibbs was a genuinely important figure in my world, the world of urban neighborhoods and urban history. In a city famous for daily destroying the memories of yesterday, she was one of the early voices for preserving city neighborhoods and honoring the city's past. And she had been a leader in the battle to turn Brooklyn Heights into the city's very first protected historic district. How could I not be excited?

I said it out loud.

"Oh, yes, she was a trailblazer in her day. That's why I tolerate her now, in spite of everything. I've known her forty years or so, and she was famous even then. That's her right there." He pointed to one of the framed photos on the wall, and I moved to see it up close. It showed a respectable-looking line of protesters, the men in suits, hats, and ties and the women in high heels and hats, holding up signs, with a tall woman leading them. Louisa Gibbs. She was a well-dressed crusader.

"She's past her demonstrating days now, though I've seen her whip out a petition in a supermarket line to demand signatures. But she's too frail for crowds, even in well-behaved meetings. She did make it to this year's holiday party though, for a little conversation and few cups of punch." He shook his head, smiling. I started to suspect that he was fond of her. "Ah, well, I'm sorry about the interruption. Let's get back to work here."

It didn't take us long. We concluded there was no one who knew what had become of that Whitman plaque. The plan was that the Nicaraguan consul would purchase it from the luncheonette owner for a reasonable price before he returned to his home in Nicaragua and then the consulate would graciously donate it back to Brooklyn. Nothing about that plan made sense to either of us, and the paper trail had no more clues.

Before I left I took one more look at the photo of Louisa Gibbs leading a demonstration, and then some of the other pictures on the wall: Margaret Truman with her father, Harry S Truman, who was then a senator, christening the battleship *Missouri* at the Brooklyn Navy Yard. Framed headlines from when the Dodgers beat the Yankees in the World Series. Fireworks at the opening of the Brooklyn Bridge. Odd, intricate drawings signed "Kingston" in flowing script.

When I left it was too late to go back to my office, and besides,

I had one more reason to walk around the neighborhood and refresh my memory about its surprises.

A little article I wrote for a local blog had caught the eye of a book editor. He emailed. Then he called. He said all things Brooklyn were hot. Neighborhood change was hot. He said I had a relatable writing style. He urged me to write a few sample chapters of a possible book. He didn't accept that I had more important things going on in my life. With his deep voice and self-assured words I pictured a middle-aged man who looked a lot like Jason Robards playing a newspaper editor in an old movie.

His name was Carter Fitzgerald III. No kidding. And I had no idea what he meant when he used words like "relatable."

Completely far-fetched? It was to me, but here was Brooklyn Heights, full of surprises, which might be a perfect subject to give it a shot. And so I took a walk.

I strolled past the spacious brick house where Truman Capote rented rooms and wrote *Breakfast at Tiffany's*. I know this partly because he wrote about the house in an article that began "I live in Brooklyn. By choice." How could I not love that? I made a little mental bow.

And the Brooklyn Women's Exchange shop was still in service, a time capsule from right out of a Louisa May Alcott book, begun before the Civil War to help indigent gentlewomen make a little money with their needlework. I was briefly distracted by the window array of dainty hand-smocked baby clothes and hand-painted ceramic tiles. This was the charming side of Brooklyn, a walk back to the days it was an independent city.

But I am a historian, after all. I know there is no place that is sheltered from changing times.

The quirky main street now had fewer offbeat local businesses than it used to, and more chain stores. Piles of dirty blankets on the sweeping limestone staircase at a large church, and in the basement entry at an apartment building, suggested homeless people were camping in the midst of all this elegance. Some posters in store windows said, "Watch out for this woman. She has been shoplifting in YOUR neighborhood shops." And others had a different photo and the heartbreaking question, "Have you seen this man? Missing from the Downtown Care Home since August. Not dangerous. Needs his meds."

This was not Brigadoon, and I knew better than to imagine that it was. I did know better. I had a fancy diploma that said so.

And then, wandering on the side streets, I realized I was on the block where Louisa Gibbs lived.

It was a leafy street where a few Edith Wharton–ish ghosts in elegant clothes might stroll, if only we could see them. Except for the tightly parked cars on both sides of a street with no driveways.

And except for the man sitting on a bench. I walked right past. I didn't even register a bundle of old clothes with—maybe—a man's head on top. Sounds cold? I'm a city girl. Sometimes we stop noticing, shameful though that is.

But he called out to me. No. It was more like a raspy whisper, but it was insistent enough to make me stop.

"Young lady," he said. "Do you happen to have anything to eat? Anything will do. Whatever you can spare." But his look at me was not as imploring as the words were. He was looking hard, right at me. It almost felt like right through me.

I did have something, a healthy protein bar in my backpack, snagged from Chris. And a bag of potato chips, all my own. I was looking forward to them in case I had an attack of munchies on the way home.

I handed both to him, carefully, to avoid touching his hands.

He smiled at me with the joy of a child and patted the bench next to hm. "Come. Sit. You have given me something I needed." He ripped the bag and popped a handful of chips into his mouth. "Let me give you something in return."

Honestly, I was repelled at the idea of taking anything he could give. His heavy winter coat was filthy, ripped at all the seams and edges. The thick scarf wrapped around his neck was full of holes.

His knitted cap was unraveling, trailing threads of yarn over his ears. And he smelled. The "war against winter" gear months too early made me wonder if he was sick.

He continued to look at me, not even sensing my discomfort. "You need a story, don't you?"

"How did you know that?" The words fell out of my mouth on their own.

"I looked at you. So we begin.

"There was a beautiful place here once. Kind people, soft voices, soft hearts. But it's all gone now, destroyed by wickedness. It was the lake that did it." He looked at me sadly. "He thought it would cleanse, but he was a fool. He did not mean it to happen. It was the demon who told him to do it."

"What lake? Is this a fairy tale?" It made no sense, but I was trying to be kind. Kinder. "From a book?"

"If you want it to be." He smiled at me. "Your story. I could tell you needed that one."

"Why are you…are you…?" I fumbled in my bag, thinking I had a bottle of water I could offer him and not knowing what else to say. "Are you all right, sitting out here?"

"Why?" He seemed surprised. "It's a bench. It's for sitting. So I sit. And I watch." He nodded, emphatically. And then he kept nodding, as if he couldn't stop. "I watch. And wait."

I handed him the water bottle. "I have to go now." I couldn't wait to get away.

"Yes. Take your story with you." He closed his eyes.

His story made no sense at all. I shrugged it off, going back to my exploration.

Yes, there was the Witnesses dormitory building, a massive modern brown brick style on a plot too small for it. It loomed over its neighbors.

And there, next to it, was an elaborate Victorian brownstone house, freestanding, with columns at the raised entrance and bay windows along the side. The stone in front was chipped in spots.

The sidewalk was cracked and heaved. How did Mrs. Gibbs with her cane manage to negotiate that? I could not see the threatened garden, though. A tall plank fence separated it from the sidewalk and ran along its side.

I was surprised when a door in the planks suddenly opened. There was Mrs. Gibbs herself with a basket of cut flowers on one arm and a cigarette in her hand. Now she wore overalls but still sported the purple sneakers.

She stopped. "I saw you with Kingston this morning. What do you want?"

Chapter Two

Ouch. I was caught in the act, snooping. So much for being the smooth professional scholar I supposedly had become. I stammered out my admiration of her work; my ownership of all her books, and how heavily annotated they were; my writing about her in school.

She stared and then smiled slightly. “I suppose you’d like to see my garden. Well, come on then.” She held the door and motioned impatiently.

It was a long strip of green grass with a flagstone pathway, a border of brilliant flowers, and a tiny tree at one end with a small table in its shade.

I don’t know a thing about gardening, but my first impression was that it was exquisite, and my second, that it was neglected. Stems poked up between the flagstone, dandelions dotted the lawn, and there were a lot of vines smothering the wooden fence.

“It’s not what it was in the days I won prizes for it.” Could she read my mind? “Oh, yes, I did. I have plaques hanging in my house. Now I’m not up to the work. I have a kid who comes to mow the lawn, and I’m not up to properly supervising him either. But now you see what I am defending.” Her sad tone became edged with anger. “Those fanatics over there?” She gestured to the tall building, visible above her fence. "Those selfish so-called believers? They want me to pull down that fence, which is all that protects me from them, and give over my perennial border. All the way to here!" She banged the cane on the spot. "To here!"

"But—I'm sorry—-I don't know the facts. How can they do that unless there are records supporting their claims?"

"Facts? Ha! Records from then are spotty, but the fact is that my great-grandfather built this house in 1875 and put in the original garden. I remember a fountain. With a dolphin, no less. The garden goes with the house and it's been here almost a century and a half. I don't care what the buyer's lawyers claim. "

She shot the modern building a venomous look and added, "He's right up there, you know."

"Who?" She couldn't mean God, could she?

"That thieving hypocrite, Daniel Towns. He has an office over there. Oh, I've been battling him forever. Did you know, when we were fighting to make this a historic district, New York's very first, Watchtower fought us at every turn?"

"Seriously? What reason could they possibly have had?" I knew what they said; I wanted to hear her interpretation.

"Oh, they weren't against it. Or rather, they couldn't have cared less either way. Cause you know, their home is not here, it is in the world to come." The sharp edge in her voice could have cut through the trunk of her garden's small tree. "What they cared about was preventing any new rules interfering with whatever they wanted to do, in perpetuity, with the property they owned and don't pay taxes on. And they own a lot." She stared hard at me. "Yes indeed. But since they use all their profits for the greater cause—you know, that invisible man in the sky—they think whatever they do is righteous. Well, I beg to differ."

I would have liked to record this whole strange interaction, or take notes, and I would, the second I was out of sight. I would do some quick research, too. I hadn't been keeping up with this issue. I had other responsibilities now.

As she eased me toward the door in the fence and lifted the lock, she said, "You are interested in this? You should meet that lovely Mr. Towns, but don't let him fool you. He's a shark, exactly like all the other big real estate businessmen."

When she turned to the door, her sunburned face turned deeper red.

"Hello, Louisa. The door was open. Did you know?"

"Mr. Towns." Her chilly tone could have frosted over the entire garden. "An open door is not the same as a welcome mat."

He nodded slightly and smiled, but not confidently. In fact he looked entirely uncomfortable, shifting his weight from side to side. His skin was shiny with sweat. "I thought there was a safety issue. Maybe you had forgotten to lock it."

"Oh, you'd like that! Old Mrs. Gibbs, getting too forgetful to manage her affairs. You could take that to court."

"Come on! We are trying hard to work with you on this issue. No one thinks you are unfit, but..." He visibly stopped himself. "But we need to get this resolved and soon. A great deal rests on it."

"Ha. A great deal for you and yours, you mean. You can sell this building and the one across the street and even keep the tunnels to connect them. A tidy package. Oh, don't look so shocked! Everyone knows about the tunnels."

I didn't. I didn't know anything about the tunnels, but now I surely wanted to.

"Louisa! Please try to see reason. Our buyer will compensate you for the loss of your garden, but he does need the entire property." I could see his hands were shaking. "It is of great importance that we get this done in timely fashion, and we are truly trying to be as accommodating as we can be."

She fixed him with a grim look. "As you always are. Good day, Daniel Towns."

He still stood in the doorway, and she closed the door in his face. He had to step back quickly to prevent damage to his nose. She slammed the lock into place with a loud clang.

I was now inside.

"Oh, damn. I forgot all about you, I was so aggravated." She held a finger to her lips and put one eye against the crack where the door hinged from the wall. "He's gone." She opened the lock again. "You step right out and get going."

I stepped out, but I didn't get going. I took my time because I could see Mr. Towns in the lobby of the building next door. I went in without thinking it through. I only knew I wanted to talk to him. I didn't exactly plan out what I would say.

I caught him as he was walking to an elevator.

"Excuse me. Mr. Towns?"

He turned, stared, said without a flicker of recognition, "Yes? Can I help you?"

"We just met. Well, not met, not exactly, but I was in Mrs. Gibbs's garden when you were there." My voice trailed off as he continued to look blankly at me. Then his expression cleared.

"Oh, yes. You are a friend of Mrs. Gibbs?" He said it very carefully. I couldn't blame him

"No, not really. I met her today for the first time. I am, uh, I am researching a little about Brooklyn Heights."

"A reporter?" He looked even more wary, and exhausted, too.

"No, no, not at all. I am a historian." I fumbled for my impressive museum business card. "Dr. Donato."

"What do you want?" Then he stopped himself. "I beg your pardon, I am being rude. It's been a difficult day. How can I help you?"

And I didn't know. I could not say, "Are you really a snake in the grass?"

"This building?" I was grasping for a subject. "It's a handsome building." Not in my opinion, but it seemed a harmless white lie. "The color fits in nicely."

"We tried hard to do that. Understand, architecture is not our goal in life, not at all, but we are nevertheless instructed to live peacefully with our neighbors if possible. Even when they persecute us, as they so often do. So we tried."

I picked up something, a touch of warmth, and made a guess. "Were you involved with this? With the planning?"

He almost smiled again. "Yes. I have been involved with our Watchtower physical plant for a long time. The sale of our buildings here, an enormous responsibility, is my last big project for my Witness family."

"I bet it's a big headache too. There is so much to do."

"We don't complain about doing our duty. Everyone does their part in our community."

I smiled at him. "What will your role be after this all moves upstate?"

Then he finally smiled back. "I will always be a faithful believer, but I will retire from this task and do whatever I am asked to do next. Pick apples, perhaps."

"Away from the big city? Won't you miss it?"

"My home in this life is wherever duty calls. Would you like to hear more about that?" He brightened. "Our beliefs about what life on earth is for? I'd be happy to share with you our blessed goals or give you some reading material to take with you."

I changed the subject as quickly as I could and not gracefully, I admit. "What did Mrs. Gibbs mean about the tunnels? Did she mean the tunnels that connect the Watchtower buildings?" I had finally remembered a reference from my long-ago research.

"Yes, she did. At least I assume she did. With that woman…" He broke off and took a breath. "Yes. We have tunnels connecting some of our buildings. It allows our workers to move quickly to assignments, no matter what the weather, and also not to crowd up the sidewalks and annoy our neighbors. Not to appear in public in sloppy or dirty work clothes. We strive for dignity at all times. And we move materials, supplies, and so on. They're efficient, brightly lit, like an office building hallway." He smiled. "In case you are imagining subway tunnels."

I sort of was, something dark and scary. Not really the Witnesses' style, I guessed. No dark places or dark deeds.

"Mrs. Gibbs? She seems so upset about all of that, your building sale here and the demands about her property." I was being vague, and I knew it. I didn't know how to say what I wanted to, which was, "Why can't you leave her alone?" She was old and frail and deeply stressed by their demands. I thought she, of all people, deserved better.

He shook his head and said, "She's always been like that, a most opinionated, aggressive woman. She scares me. I'm not used to... Women don't...in our life..." He stopped as suddenly as he had started, looking shocked by his own rambling words. "She threatened to shoot me recently. She is a madwoman, and in her madness, she has become yet another persecutor of our faith. Like the Russians, who are more vicious than ever." He stopped himself and then added quickly, "On a smaller scale, I should admit. But sadly the hatred of us never really ends." He hastily turned toward the elevator. His parting words, "Good day, miss. I need to lie down now," floated back to me over his shoulder.

The chance to talk further was gone. There was nothing else for me to do here, but there were many things to do when I got home. Make notes for work about the seemingly lost-forever Whitman plaque. Make some notes for myself about the puzzling people I had met today, and learn a little more if I could. I should think seriously about starting that sample chapter. I'd just do a quick search to shine some light on today's surprises.

Seriously? I should have known better. I became glued to my screen, generating dozens of news items: people who were apprehensive about all the real estate about to be sold to private developers, much of it right on the borders of the historic district. On the wrong side? How would it change, well, everything? Disturbing a balance of many decades standing. Some people said good riddance, the Watchtower Society never cared about the neighborhood anyway, and were not susceptible to local pressure. As one interviewee said, quoting an old ad for kosher hot dogs, "They think they answer to a higher authority." Some said they had been good neighbors, better than floods of yuppies in expensive apartments would be.

Good thing my daughter Chris grabbed a bite after basketball practice and Joe, the man in my life, was on a job and coming home late. I had a few hours of work still ahead of me to update my knowledge. Call me crazy. Or insecure. Or maybe, to tell the truth, just plain curious.

I guess I fell asleep at the keyboard. Chris found me, woke me, and sent me to bed.

Chapter Three

Later I thought about how I'd met Louisa Gibbs. It was a lot like the time I saw a famous rock star riffing with a street musician. Once in a lifetime.

Could she be persuaded to let me sit at her feet and listen to all her stories? That would be the book chapter I should write.

And then I didn't have to persuade her. There she was, on the other end of the telephone, her worn, smoky voice inviting me to tea.

"Whatever you are writing about Brooklyn Heights, if you want to get it right, you need to talk to me." Yes, indeed. "Come at three tomorrow." And then she hung up. I had not said a word.

I was certainly excited. The student I used to be could not believe her luck. I was also annoyed, as the employed parent I am now had other responsibilities. Part of me wanted to call her back and have a discussion about manners and respect, but that was certainly a fantasy. I knew I would go. I could call it a research afternoon, and no one would actually question that. I hoped. I was still getting used to living in the nine-to-five world. Wasn't this part of my job?

Next day, there I was, working the tarnished brass ship door knocker and dressed like a lady, or as close as I could get. My best-looking pants and a fit-for-work blazer would have to be good enough for this occasion. And Chris contributed a real purse I didn't even know she had, to replace my usual backpack. As usual, there was a comment too. "Keep it. You need to upgrade your look, Dr. Mom."

I waited. And waited. The massive door was finally opened by a very young woman with blue streaks in her dark hair and a neck covered with twining blue tattoos. The hands holding the door open were adorned with Indian henna patterns.

"You Professor Donato? I'm Sierra. Sorry it took so long. I was helping Louisa down the steps."

I managed to smother my surprise. At least I hoped I did.

In a large front room with a big bay window overlooking the street, a low table was set between two chintz-covered armchairs. It held a silver tray with a flowery china teapot, matching delicate china cups, and a tiered stand with tiny sandwiches and cookies. I moved carefully, terrified of breaking something.

Louisa smiled. "Welcome, Dr. Donato. Sierra, this looks lovely."

The table did, but Sierra's shorts and her sandals, with grubby toes and multicolored nails peeping out, were a startling mismatch on the beautiful, faded rug.

"Okay to go? I don't think I forgot anything."

"Ah, yes, we are taken care of. You go on." She turned to me. "I find I need a light snack in the afternoon. Will you pour? My hands have become a bit shaky."

I'd watched British dramas on public television. Surely I could fake graciously pouring a cup of tea while I ate a dainty sandwich or three? I did my best.

Mrs. Gibbs sucked down her tea in a few sips, and her sandwiches disappeared in two bites each. "Kingston tells me you are writing about Brooklyn Heights and that you are a certified historian. Is that correct?'

"If by certified you mean I have a degree, then yes, I am. I have a PhD in urban history. Actually, my specialty is Brooklyn."

"Ah. Then I have some interesting stories to tell you and things to show you. A lot of them, plus this house itself."

I could not believe my luck. And I should not have, because this was not a gift.

"I want something from you. Did you think I talk to everyone out of the goodness of my heart? I have good qualities, but that is not one of them. This is one hand washing the other. You may have heard I am in a dispute with my neighbors, those Bible-thumpers?" Her sly glance told me she was joking. She had not forgotten that I had witnessed her encounter with Kingston.

"I may be forced into court. Probably I will be. So if I need your help, can I count on you? You could do some research for me, tell my story from an objective point of view, because they don't accept me as reliable. What nerve!"

"Do you mean tell them what you want them to hear?"

"Absolutely! What would be the point of asking you, otherwise?" My face must have shown my horrified reaction. "Dear, dear! You look upset. I am not suggesting you lie. Can't do that if you are a scholar, right? But I have confidence I am right, so what you find can only help me!

"We can have a house tour right now." She used her cane to stand up, and then used it as a pointer. "Built by my great-grandfather after he made a fortune in the China trade. He could see his ships down in the harbor from his front steps in those days, according to family legend anyway. The house has barely been changed since then."

She made a sweeping gesture that encompassed the entire first floor. "However, my mother insisted on a Frigidaire, and my father updated the bathrooms. Now, one more cookie for me, and then we walk around. And do tell me more about this article Kingston mentioned? Are you writing one?"

"Maybe. There's an editor who wants me to write a few sample chapters for a book proposal. It's a long shot, in my opinion.

Plus I had a chapter in my dissertation about creating the historic district, and I'm thinking it's time to update it."

"You think anything has changed?"

It took me a minute to catch on that was a joke.

"Then you certainly need my help. You know you cannot always get it right from the official story." She gave me a shrewd look. "Did you mention me back then?"

"I most certainly did."

Her smile was satisfied and even smug.

We toured the parlor floor of her home, with its dark wood paneling, faded silk furniture, and a baby grand piano. I admired the antique wallpaper, a beautiful painted harbor scene with tall ships—was it New York Harbor, right down the hill from where we stood?—and wondered what used to be in my own house. Everything original had been long gone when I moved in.

"The garden floor is not authentic, so we won't bother with that. Equipment in the kitchen down there has been replaced as it wore out." She shook her head. "Rather like bodies. I have two titanium hips myself. Anyway, I cannot get people to work for me without having modern appliances."

She waved a dismissive hand. "And who can blame them? My mother would be horrified, but this is not 1920, when there were two live-in maids, a cook, and a driver, all working for pennies, no doubt. They lived in tiny cubicles on the top floor." She shook her head. "It's storage now. And my girl thinks we should get something called Wi-Fi! She's teaching me how to use email."

We returned to the chairs in the parlor. "So. My papers are with Kingston in the association archives, but I have stories, too." She winked. "And gossip. You come again and we can get down to work. A deal?"

I agreed. I wanted to know more, but I was now almost late for a parent meeting at Chris's school.

Twenty minutes later I slipped into a crowded meeting room to find my anxious daughter saving me a seat.

The speakers for this meeting were introduced, and I started to take notes, then nudged my kid and whispered, "You should be taking notes too. Your life."

She pulled out her phone to tap info into it, while I used my notebook. She often accuses me of living in the past. I do, and I'm proud of it. I am a historian, after all.

The school's college counselor spoke first. Three alums spoke about the college admissions process from their own experiences and described how they ended up where they did.

When an independent college admissions adviser was introduced, I wondered why parents at this costly private school would pay for extra help. And how could they?

But what did I know, anyway? I went to a giant public high school with overwhelmed counselors and then went to Brooklyn College, practically across the street. I slept in my childhood bedroom and took the same old city bus to classes.

When Chris was little and I was a widowed mom, back in school myself, I needed the extended childcare a private school offered. My husband's life insurance made it financially possible, barely. Then they offered us substantial financial aid, and she was flourishing there, so she stayed.

And now? Now she had big ideas about her future. I wondered, not for the first time, if it had all been a mistake.

When I tried to talk to her about tuition costs and travel costs and hometown colleges, she wasn't listening. I could see the thought bubbles over her head. "Blah blah blah."

I foresaw a long year ahead. And I wondered if Joe, now a quasi-stepdad, realized what he was in for. When we got home, though, I saw his experience was going to be different from mine.

"Joe! It was such a great meeting!" Funny she talked to him when she wouldn't talk to me. Not so funny. "We learned so much. And they had a kid talking about Oberlin." She added, almost whispering, "It's my dream. I talked to him after. He gave me lot of good tips." She turned pink. "Jared is definitely going. Early admission."

Joe saw my face and winked at me behind Chris's back. I should be glad she had an adult she found so easy to talk to, even if it wasn't me. And I *was* glad. Usually.

She went off for a snack, and he put his arms around me.

"It'll be fine. You know that."

"How do you know? There is the money to worry about. She should be thinking about the state university arts college. And Jared! I mean, he is a nice kid, but he's a kid. And so is she. What if she follows him and they break up? And..."

He put a finger to my lips.

"I know, because I have six nieces and nephews who went through this. Count 'em. Six. And Chris is smart and talented. She'll get scholarships like always. And by application time next year, maybe Jared will be out of the picture anyway."

I stood there, leaning on his comforting shoulder, trying to process this too-full day. I knew I'd have to find a way to say some things to Chris she would not want to hear, but I had no idea how. Not tonight anyway.

Over a glass of wine, stretched out on the couch, Joe and I caught up on the rest of the day. I told him maybe I really would try to write that sample chapter, that I'd had a story fall into my lap today.

He started laughing.

"What?" I was exasperated. He had a great laugh, but it wasn't so charming at that moment. "What in the world?"

"I have a cocktail party tomorrow. You, my dear, flatly refused to come with. Remember? Not your people and not your style?"

"Uh, yes. Maybe that happened."

"Maybe? Housewarming at a client's? I managed a big renovation? Remember where?"

The light was dawning. Brooklyn Heights.

"And who? A big shot? With money?"

"Lucky guess. You maybe have heard of Prince Projects?"

Oh, yes, I had. I'd seen it on many construction site billboards too.

"He's buying and building. He's deeply involved in some pieces of the Watchtower transfers in the Heights. The party's a political fund-raiser. They'll all be there, all the movers and shakers." He was laughing at me. "Care to change your mind?"

"Please? Could I please change my mind? I'll check if my good dress is pressed?"

"You'd be cute even in blue jeans. And by the way, their name is really Prinzig, not Prince."

Interesting. Did Prinzig not sound elegant enough?

Chapter Four

A party? Yes, I dimly remembered declining Joe's original invitation with a faint feeling of horror. All I heard was a weeknight evening—I am too busy, too tired—with people who did not interest me, rich dwellers in the business world.

And I'd have to dress up. It's not that I deeply dislike doing that, but years of minimal social life and not enough money to buy clothes anyway, had removed it from my skill set. I hadn't known how to do it since that long-ago era of off-the-shoulder sweatshirts and fluffy hair.

But now I could do this. I could. I said that to myself a few times. I had a reason to be there, so I would not merely be Joe's date, a sort of arm candy. I'd be going to learn something if I could, and I was pretty good at that role.

And I had a dress. Darcy, my most stylish friend, had dragged me shopping before Chris's sweet sixteen party. Shimmery silk with a few strategic rhinestones and color-coordinated, glittery high heels. Chris insisted I leave my hair and makeup to her.

Actually, what she said was, "Don't even think about your eyeliner. I'm on it. Mel will help." She giggled. "Cinderella to the ball."

I huffed and protested it was a cocktail party, not even close to a ball, but she rudely put her hands over her ears while saying, "You have to leave it to us."

So I did. When they turned me to the mirror, I was shocked. I looked glamorous. Or at least polished and glowy, compared to my everyday self. Joe said, "Wow," and I asked stupidly, "Is this what you'd like me to be all the time? Glammed up instead of everyday scruffy me?" I instantly regretted it.

"You're kidding, right? Your real self is the one I want to come home to every night." He stopped right in the street and put his hands on my shoulders. "You know I can't resist that scruffy you."

Yes, I had the right guy.

We went in style, taking a car service so we did not have drinking-and-driving issues later. And parking issues. The party was in a former factory building, down the hill from Brooklyn Heights itself. That former factory was converted into million-dollar loft apartments. Joe corrected me. *Several*-million-dollar loft apartments.

The elevator opened directly into an apartment foyer on the top floor. It was a lot of space, the true luxury in our land-scarce city. Long open rooms with huge factory-style windows overlooking the harbor. Huge abstract paintings on the towering walls impressed but puzzled me. Soft jazz came from a quartet in a corner. A uniformed team checked our names and took our coats. Servers moved smoothly across the polished floors, offering trays of wine and tiny bites of things I could not identify. Even with the many servers and the large, glittery crowd of guests, the rooms were not crowded.

What was I doing here? A girl from deepest Brooklyn? In this movie star setting? Why, accepting a flute of champagne, thank you very much, and hoping my lipstick would not smear on the crystal. That's what.

I was here to do a job. Meet some people who could talk to me about their world. This world. Joe winked. He could read my mind.

"Remind me. How do you know these people? You worked here?"

"For a full year, on and off." He smiled at me. "In the co-op they bought fully renovated." Now he was all but laughing. "Oh, yeah. After they moved in, they decided the three bathrooms weren't grand enough for their needs and I was general contractor for the Italian mosaic retiling, the rainfall showers, and a Jacuzzi. Plus the self-watering for the patio garden and the complete landscaping. They trusted me because—I don't know. I can read and understand a contract? I speak grammatical English and know the names of furniture designers? That table over there is a genuine Nakashima, by the way."

I knew the name, but only because I'd seen Nakashima's work on *Antiques Roadshow*. I felt like Eliza Doolittle on her first day at Professor Higgins's house. A long way from home.

Joe nudged me toward the French doors at the end of the long living room. A redwood deck outside that seemed to be the square footage of my entire first floor. Three levels and planters with manicured trees now turning autumn gold.

"I can see you liked working for them a whole lot." My turn to tease him.

"My job is making clients happy. They don't have to make me happy in any way but paying my bills. Some I like less than others." He turned me slightly, "And there they are. These clients. Come meet them." He removed the glass of champagne from my hand and whispered as we walked, "He is buying a chunk of the Watchtower properties. So you need to be alert and analytical, right? Name is Mike Prinzig. Of Prince Projects. That guy. And his wife, Cherie."

Mike Prinzig was a not-quite-handsome man with slick, styled black hair and too many shiny teeth, standing with a very blond woman in heels about five inches higher than mine. They smiled as we approached. He shook Joe's hand and put an arm around his shoulders while still holding a cocktail glass. She kissed Joe—was that a little too friendly?—and said, "We miss seeing you over breakfast!" That was definitely too friendly from this six-foot blond.

He introduced me, smoothly slipped in my not exactly real experience writing on Brooklyn Heights, and kept a hand on my bare shoulder in a way that said a lot with no words at all.

Mike Prinzig said, "Well, I know Brooklyn Heights in and out. Come talk to me sometime to get an expert view."

Cocktails were pressed into our hands, and the lady of the house was saying, "We're thinking of updating the kitchen." She looked around with a dissatisfied expression. "This big party shows me it is not quite up to the entertaining we plan to do. Right, honey?" She leaned on her husband's arm.

"You are the party expert. If it needs tweaking, then why not? So, Joe, we'll talk? Next week sometime? Call my girl." They turned to greet other guests, and Joe managed to walk me away before I said anything.

I started to laugh, but he said, "This is how it works. Some networking needs to be done. Not a word until we get home. Not a word. But yes, not people I'd like for friends. However, he's rebuilding half of Brooklyn Heights, including most of the block where your new friend lives."

I stopped laughing.

"He's too busy hosting to be useful tonight—I should have expected that—but there's someone else you should meet."

"I'm listening."

"Okay, don't turn around, but in the corner is his old man, the first Prinzig tycoon. I've worked for him, too, and he's a little less, say, diplomatic. With any luck, he's been drinking, too. And he looks like he'd like some company."

He was an old man, bald, more like two generations from his son than one. He sat at his perch next to a small table, looking over the crowded room with a sharp eye. I had the immediate thought that he didn't miss a thing. He had a half-empty bottle of rye on his table and a half-empty glass in his hand. It was a nice party, but he didn't look as if he was having much fun.

"Mr. Prinzig? How are you tonight? Joe Greenberg. We met..."

"I remember you. The sugar factory conversion. Good work, tough negotiations."

Joe smiled. "I'll take that as a compliment."

"And so it's meant, as long as you are not negotiating opposite me. You worked on this place? For my idiot son? The guy who took the family name off the company. Hope you skinned him real good on your work." His smile was oddly satisfied. "And his party-girl wife. I warned him about her, having some experiences in that type of relationship." He took a long pull on his drink and then noticed me. "But I am being rude. Who is this young lady in the elegant high heels?"

"This is Erica Donato. She is a good friend of mine who was anxious to meet you. Be nice to her; the shoes are painful."

"And why would that be? Meeting me, not the shoes? Though they are most becoming."

I sent a look to Joe that was meant to say, "What are we doing here?" Joe responded by hooking a reassuring hand around my elbow.

"She is working on a story about Brooklyn Heights, and I knew you would be a great source."

"A reporter? I never talk to them. They're always looking for the story that bleeds. Bloodsuckers."

"No, not at all." I spoke up for myself. "I'm a historian, and I'm looking at..." I thought fast. I didn't know yet what I wanted. "...I'm looking at some of what made the neighborhood what it is today. It's come a long way from the downhill slide of the sixties, right?"

Oh, yes, all true, but as vague as it could get. It would be true of many neighborhoods.

"Come with me." He threaded his way through the crowd, glass in one hand and bottle in the other, to the French doors and then out to the terrace.

"Beautiful layout, beautiful view." Joe, appraising professionally.

"Nonsense. They'll never use it, and the staggering cost could have been invested. Forget that. Look over there."

He pointed back up the hill that gave the Heights its name, toward a group of tall buildings along the border, just outside the landmarked district. "See those? I built them. You betcha, the neighborhood was going right downhill then. That was the beginning of the comeback. When people say renewal, young lady, you have to thank me, not these Johnny-come-latelies." He named a few, including his son, and some of them had been around for a couple of decades already. Not so lately.

"I could have done a lot more. All that growth that's going on now? Those were my ideas! But we could only go so far then. There was a community of airheads and do-gooders who thought they had something to say."

I muffled my own thoughts and looked at Joe, whose eyes were sparking back at me.

"Do you mean people like Louisa Gibbs?"

"Not *like* her. I mean her, herself. A born rabble-rouser. Yeah, yeah, so they were educated rabble? So what? What a pain that woman was! And still is. I was tempted, plenty of times…" The hand that was holding the glass clenched into a fist so fiercely the glass shook. "Well, she's getting what's coming to her, and my son of all people is making it happen."

"Do tell me more." I even tried to look enthusiastic. I was getting the hang of this conversation.

"He's picking off some of the smaller buildings the Witnesses are selling. That's no secret. And they happen to surround that old house of hers." He smiled and smacked his bottle down on the table. "Bam! Bam! Bam! By the time he is done renovating, she'll be happy to sell him that old pile of stone for a couple of bucks."

What was he saying? And did he even know what he was talking about? I had so many questions, all indiscreet and inappropriate for this party, I did not know what to ask first. Joe stepped in.

"Impressive. I hadn't picked up on that plan." He looked interested. "I only heard there was a small dispute over a property line." He winked at me. "He wants it all? But the whole street is landmarked. What can he possibly do to her?"

"Ah, children, you have no idea how construction can be drawn out. And you a contractor yourself." He gave Joe a friendly punch on the arm. "You must be an honest one. Trust me, by the time the endless noise and traffic on that street lasts a year or so, and he's also got a couple of lawsuits in the works, little old Louisa will be happy to give it up. And if she isn't, he has other plans to discourage her. My son isn't always the brightest bulb, but he's got that idea nailed down." He settled into the nearest chair and motioned to a waiter for another bottle. "Of course, he learned it all from me. See, I taught him there is always a way." He took a long pull on the liquor. "And then there are other ways."

Another old man drifted up and shook his hand, and Joe said loudly, "Come on, honey, let's get some refills," and steered me safely toward the bar before I could tell the senior Mr. Prinzig what I thought of him.

Out of his hearing, Joe whispered, "Time for Cinderella to get home and to bed."

"But I wanted to ask him more questions. How could he think he could get away with that? And is his son really planning it, or is he delusional? Is..."

Joe looked amused, but he was not making it easy to return to that corner of the room. "It wasn't a question. It's time to go home. One, because I know this guy, and you don't want to set him off at a social event. Where, by the way, I have many customers."

"Oh. Right."

"And two, my lovely hothead, don't you think you might want to come back to these jerks with more questions later?"

I had to concede on that.

"And three, because this is a fund-raiser, and they are auctioning art way beyond our price range."

Anything would be beyond my price range.

"So let's get out of here before it starts, OK?"

"OK." Suddenly I was very tired, at the end of a long, full day. And perhaps a little drunk. "I won't burn any bridges tonight." Another night, who knows?

It took a while to work our way through the crowd. Joe knew so many people there, and they all seemed glad to see him. Handshakes were exchanged, information and gossip shared. He was very smooth, my Joe, and highly respected. I hadn't seen him in this setting before. I was impressed.

When I took one last glance back at the hosts, I was astonished to see Dr. Kingston standing in a secluded corner, deep in conversation with Mike Prinzig. Of all people, those were two I could never have imagined at the same party at all, yet there they were, talking away. Dr. Kingston said something Prinzig liked. He nodded, laughed, smiled. He lifted his glass to Dr. Kingston, who lifted his back.

I leaned on Joe's arm, nudging him in their direction.

"I don't get that. That's Dr. Kingston. I told you about him. They should be natural enemies. They'd disagree about every single thing."

"Think, sweetie. It's politics. You fight it out on one thing, but maybe the next, you could be allies. I'm guessing that this Kingston always needs money for his civic causes, right?"

I nodded. That was likely.

"And I know Mike is desperate to be respected, to be considered someone."

"A contender?"

Joe got the reference and smiled. "Exactly. So what's the shortcut in our great city?"

"Ah. Now I get it. Give big to good causes. Make a name that way."

I never got back to talk to him. The elevator doors opened for us, and out came a stocky woman whose hair looked as if she cut it herself. Her all-black outfit was barely a notch above blue jeans. Not stylish jeans, working jeans.

Joe said, "Nancy! I didn't expect to see you here."

"You got that right. Not really my kind of party. I was persuaded I should show up for a hot minute or two."

"You worked here, too? We never stumbled over each other."

"Not here, but one of the hotels he bought."

"That was you? I was too busy to bid on that job." Joe introduced us and added, "Nancy is one of the top restoration experts around here. In fact—do I have this right?" He turned to her. "You worked on that McWilliams-Gibbs mansion?"

"Sure did. Me and Louisa go back so far, one winter her work was all that kept me going."

That got my attention.

"I visited her the other day. The house is amazing, really special."

She nodded. "I don't take every job these days, only if I like the people a lot or the house is special."

"And with Mrs. Gibbs?'

"Oh, both!" She laughed. "Both. Always an interesting and complex problem to make the building stable but keep it pretty. And I get such a charge out of Louisa." She stopped for a moment. "She's like the eccentric old aunt I should have had. So I keep going back, in spite of the location."

Soon she went off to, as she said, shake hands and be visible, and we caught the elevator door next time it opened.

I fell asleep on the short cab ride home. Upstairs in a fog, bed in a T-shirt, restless dreams of construction noises and printed words repeating "location—location—location," until I fell into a dream of arms around me.

Chapter Five

In the morning I still had no idea about how to proceed with my kid or how to make the best use of the people I had met at that party, but I had a desk full of work. I would need to set Brooklyn Heights aside for now.

Someone up there was laughing when I said that to myself, but I didn't know it then. At that moment I did shove the Heights to the back of my mind like an old artifact in a storeroom and spent the day dealing with real artifacts in real storerooms.

Hours later, exploring the storeroom had produced some intriguing pieces that did not seem to have any identifying information. I started from the assumption that that was impossible and got to work in the relevant record systems. It kept me busy all afternoon.

That night a sound woke me out of a deep sleep. A phone was ringing. House? Cell? It was dark, predawn dark. I squinted, groped, found the offending gadget. Could not read the calling number.

"Hello" came out as "Huh?" It was not Chris, who was at home. Better be at home and in bed. Not Joe, who was at his own place tonight. Not Dad. A wavering voice. "Please help. I don't know what to do."

"Hello? Who?" That was the best I could do until my eyes stayed open.

More firmly. "It is Louisa. I am sorry to call so late, but… but…I could not reach Sierra. Or a neighbor. Anyone." Her voice dropped to a whisper. "So many are gone now. My neighbors. Dead. Or moved to Florida." Then she came back with, "Your card was right there. You seemed to be a quite capable young woman. I need. I need some help. The police…"

That shocked me into consciousness. "Now? At this hour?"

"No, not now. It's the middle of the night. I talked to them earlier. They had questions. And now I cannot sleep no matter what I do."

"Mrs. Gibbs. What in the world?"

"Ah. I see I am not explaining. They had questions for me." There was a long pause, so long my eyes started to close. "I am getting these letters."

"What letters?" I tried to wake up my brain. "About your property line?"

"No. No. That would be bad enough, but no. These are, well, they are personal. Angry. They threaten."

"I see." Did I? No. Not at all. "What are you saying? What kind of threats?"

"Vague, but someone doesn't like me." She gave a completely phony laugh. "Really doesn't like me. And tells me so."

"And you talked to the police about it?" It was finally sinking in.

"I am to go in to see them. Tomorrow. No, now it's today." There was a long pause. "I am so sorry, Ms. Donato. I mean Dr. Donato. I don't know what I was thinking to call you like this. I, well, I was all right earlier, but I woke up confused in the night. Do you ever have that, middle-of-the-night panic?"

"I did. I do. I understand." I would not tell her how well I understood. "It's all right. Are you better now?"

"Yes, I believe I am. Again, I am sorry." She sounded firmer.

Sleepy but clear. "It all seems different in the dawn, doesn't it? I'll manage. Thank you for your time, dear. Good night."

A soft click of the phone and she was gone. She sounded reassured just from saying it all out loud. I certainly had not said anything useful. And now I was fully wide awake at 4:00 a.m. A mug of warm milk with a shot of whiskey added would put me back to sleep. Maybe. And then would I be able to get up for work? I decided to settle for cocoa and a slice of toast.

It made me feel better, but it did not stop the questions from tumbling through my mind. I was well and truly awake.

As excited as I had been to meet the great Louisa Gibbs, I didn't know much about her. Not really. Her public life, but not who she was. Maybe some answers would turn my mind to Off and let me catch a few more hours of sleep.

I moved around as quietly as I could and went to my desk. Lights off. Only the screen was on, but it was enough.

I already knew about Mrs. Gibbs's great-grandfather, who had made the first fortune, but now I learned about a grandfather who added to it with real estate development as Brooklyn grew and grew.

Her own father, inheriting two fortunes, had done not much of anything, it seemed. He was described as a sportsman and clubman, whatever that meant. Did he spend his life playing?

He married a woman with a Dutch name who was indeed a descendent of the early Dutch settlers and had danced with young Franklin Roosevelt, that most famous Dutch descendent, at society balls.

And along came little Louisa, who insisted on being called Louie and refused to be a proper young deb. She had lobbied for Vassar until she wore her parents down, then spent her twenties on a suitable marriage that went bad in a few years. There was another, most unsuitable one, which also went bad. She never had children. And then her devotion to her home and neighborhood and to many causes in addition to preservation. She certainly had an interesting life.

And I was still not asleep. I crawled back to bed, thinking with some satisfaction that I had another source for Brooklyn stories, my own confidential informant. It was time for a call to my friend Leary. In the morning.

I was sure that strange phone call would keep me up anyway, but next thing I knew, it was daylight, and I'd slept through the alarm. I sprang into action before I was fully functioning, splashed water in my face, and grabbed my work clothes from the day before. I'd get coffee at work and tough out no breakfast, unless I got lucky and found a street cart with doughnuts at the museum parking lot. No time to walk over today. It's a long walk and longer two-bus ride, but a five-minute drive.

I found Chris in the kitchen.

"Where's Joe this morning?"

"He stayed at his own place because of an early appointment."

"What? No one to make me breakfast?" Her grin was full of mischief.

"You can have dry cereal and raisins." It's true; Joe is a better cook than I am. "You are quite capable of making that yourself."

"I know, I know." She gave me a quick hug. "But I'm getting to depend on his egg sandwiches. Remember, I'm a growing girl."

I thought about her words even as I hustled to my car on the street and wove through the morning traffic. She seemed to have adjusted to Joe's regular presence pretty well. Very well. She doesn't remember her father at all. I often thought Joe filled that space for her all along, even though I had always assured her that we were a perfect team of two.

As my relationship with Joe grew from long friendship to something more intense, I had worried about it. There was a lot of tiptoeing around it, sneaking around it, too, to tell the truth.

When it was finally time to let Chris see that Joe spent some nights, I was so nervous I could not sleep. When Joe joined us for breakfast in pajamas, Chris barely blinked. Later, turning red,

I'm sure, I said, "So now you know Joe and I have a—a romantic relationship."

She gave me one of those scornful looks teenagers do so expertly. "Well, I've heard of sex. What took you so long to admit it?"

"What are you talking about?"

She said it out loud, slowly. "Mom, I am not an idiot. I knew it all along. Even before you did." Then she returned to her texting. As simple as that. A minefield safely crossed. That's how I felt.

I didn't remember the middle-of-the-night call until I was pulling into the museum parking lot. Damn. Not shaping up to be a good day.

As soon as I had a free minute, I called Leary. He was a grouchy retired reporter who had been on the Brooklyn beat for many decades, until his drinking and diabetes caught up with him. To hear him tell it, if there was something about Brooklyn he didn't know, it wasn't worth knowing. That might even be true.

He claimed not to be lonely or need company but that was, I'd come to realize, not even close to true. I could usually pry open his memory by being there and listening with admiration. The admiration was real. The food I bring helps prime the pump.

I called, expecting his usual grumbling and ready to ask if he'd like pasta or Chinese tonight.

"Not tonight, kiddo. Not convenient."

"Do you have a sports-watching date with my dad?" They had developed an unlikely friendship that made me uncomfortable. They'd met through me, so I had only myself to blame. "Is it football season already?"

I could feel him smiling right through the phone. "Do you think he is my only friend?"

Yes, I did think exactly that. He was not exactly a friendly guy.

"It's a surprise that you have any old friends. So can I quick, ask you what you know about Brooklyn Heights history about mid-twentieth-century?"

"You been reading up on it? Neighborhood papers? I wrote

most of those articles." He sounded insulted. "Covered the whole story of the establishment of the historic district and after. Course I was no more than a kid at the time. The Moses plans, building the promenade, the whole deal. On and off. You know, there were always disagreements. Very politically aroused, those rehabbing brownstoners were then. I believe the current term is 'woke.'"

"How the heck did you know that?"

"You underestimate me."

"Did you ever meet Louisa Gibbs? She was an important leader in…"

"Are you kidding? Yes, I know who she is. I knew her, too, and still do. No one better. You couldn't miss her, covering that beat! We are having dinner tonight."

"No!"

"We do that a couple times a year. Like I said, I knew her well, back then."

"What was she like?"

"Are you saying, 'Tell me about the old days, Grandpa?'"

"You bet."

"Yeah, OK. She was a force of nature. Seriously. Lit up a crowd. It was, some of it was, family pride, I guess, but she was clear about what makes a neighborhood and why it mattered to her. Turned out, it mattered to a lot of people."

"You liked her!" He didn't like many people.

"To tell the truth, I never met anyone like her, then or since. You want to join us for dinner? Can't talk more now. Got to run." He chuckled as he was putting the phone down. He had lost a leg to diabetes, and there was no running in his life. It was what he called "cripple humor," the kind of joke he could make but any other person had better not even try. You'd regret it.

As to Louisa, I'd call her back as soon as I had a minute to check on her She had sounded shaky, not at all like Louisa the famous activist.

As it turned out it was almost lunchtime before I had that

moment to breathe. The number I called rang and rang, but no one picked up, and no answering machine answered. I thought it was her house phone, but I had another number, too. A cell? She had a cell phone?

When she answered, and I asked her that, she snapped, "Do you think I live in the Dark Ages?"

I was glad she could not see my embarrassed face. I very tentatively asked how she was doing.

"Outraged. That is how I am right now. Those cops insisted I come to the precinct today. I am outside now, waiting for a car to take me there. "

"Did you reach someone? Dr. Kingston? Or do you at least have your aide—is it Sierra?—with you?"

"What? Am I a child?" The real Louisa was definitely back. "I can handle a few questions without a babysitter." She was back and then some.

I looked at the clock. I had my car, I had some time for lunch, I knew where the precinct was and had a few shortcuts to get over there. I had learned some useful things from my dad, the retired cabbie.

Big breath. "Would you like me to meet you there? To have another set of eyes and ears?"

There was a long silence. "If you want to." Another silence. "Do you doubt I can still manage a few wet-behind-the-ears civil servants on my own? You forget I battled Robert Moses."

How did she know the cops were young? Oh, of course. To her, everyone was young. I wondered why she was so belligerent.

I zipped over to the precinct and found her in the reception area.

"After they insisted I come here, they are not ready for me. What rudeness!" Her face was set and angry, but her eyes were something else. "And this coffee is vile."

"I can't help that, but I might have a cookie in my purse."

"Ah, yes."

Before I found it, we had a man in plain clothes in front of us. And yeah, he certainly did look like a kid disguised in a suit.

"Mrs. Gibbs, thank you for coming in. I'm Detective Kahn. I'll take you back to meet Sergeant Torres."

When I stood up, too, he said, "Your lawyer? Really, you did not need one. You are only here to give us some more information."

"She's not a lawyer, she's a friend. She is here to help me."

"No. We need to have privacy for this. No distractions."

She stopped and planted her cane firmly on the worn linoleum. "Then I'm not going anywhere. I am far too old to be subjected to this without some moral support." She looked as stubborn as she sounded. That is, until he turned away for a moment, and she winked at me. "If I had a health aide with me, you'd let her in, wouldn't you? Or a service animal?"

He'd been outgunned. He didn't say another word, just silently motioned us both to follow him.

Sergeant Torres was a mature woman, older than me. My immediate impression was that she was tall and attractive and that she dressed drably, gray slacks, plain buttoned business shirt, dark blazer. Blond hair pinned into a tight bun. Was she trying to hide her good looks while on the job?

Louisa spoke up immediately. "Why on earth did you drag me here? Those threatening letters? You could have come to me. This is not supportive. It feels like I am the one being questioned."

The two detectives exchanged looks, and Torres, unruffled, said, "Not at all. We merely find that people have, ah, more complete information when they come here. And did you bring us your letters?"

She sat completely still for a moment, then reached into her enormous purse and slapped some envelopes down on the desk. "Here. All of them." She took a deep breath as she kept her hand on the papers. "I have been worried, but I told no one. I am not one to scare easily." Her expression was fierce, but I saw her hand trembling. She quickly clasped her other hand over it so they both rested on the envelopes. "I have had four letters, unsigned, making threats. It's not hard to find the motives for that."

She slid them across the desk to the sergeant.

"We will keep them, look at them, and certainly handle them very carefully. We may need them for analysis, depending on what happens. Would you like us to make you copies? Now, tell us again how they came to you. Do you know when?"

"I found them early in the morning, on the floor of my foyer, put through the mail slot in the door. Someone in the night, but I never saw anyone."

"Do you know when?"

"The last two weeks. I thought the first was some evil prank. Evil but not important. But then there were more. They wish to scare me, I believe."

Her voice was firm, but her hand was trembling again. I put mine out to cover it.

The young officer was recording. The sergeant asked, "Who is the 'they'?"

"Oh, please! Aren't you up on local politics? That builder who is buying up the property around me? Prinzig? Prince is the company name. And the Watchtower gang that is selling it? Yes, I called them a gang. They are tormenting me. They have been for some time."

The expression on Sergeant Torres's face was odd. Though she'd asked the question, she did not seem surprised at the answer. Mostly she appeared unimpressed and watchful. I wondered what she already knew.

"There is more. " The sergeant spoke very carefully. "We have some additional questions for you."

Louisa stared back at her, unflinching, angry.

"Do you know a Daniel Towns?"

"Know him? He is behind the legal papers they are throwing at me. He is very anxious for the sale to be settled. We have had a long…"

I squeezed her hand, hoping she would pick up that I was telling her to stop. She closed her mouth tightly.

"Well, there is a problem with your accusations. Mr. Towns is getting angry anonymous letters, too."

Louisa was stunned into silence. I was too. When we recovered, we started at once.

"That is not possible."

"But who? Why? Towns? I don't..."

The officers sat still, watching, as our voices faded.

"We'd like to know, too, but we can't answer any of those questions, not yet. We're working on it, and that's one reason you are here. We have a handwriting analyst. That is our plan for today, to do some testing regarding the letters to Mr. Towns. Fortunately, she can look over yours, too, and see what we learn."

She nodded, and Detective Kahn opened the office door. "We need some official handwriting samples taken from you. It will only require a few minutes. We brought someone in to do that today. Will you give us some samples?"

Louisa turned white. Her hand under my mine started shaking again.

"No. I won't. This is an invasion of my privacy and legally questionable. I did some research."

"Louisa?" I responded before I remembered my promise to keep quiet.

"When I couldn't sleep last night, worrying about my own letters?" She looked up at me, half-proud, and half—could it be embarrassed? "I used that Google thing to look up how these kind of stupid, horrible letters get investigated. There have been legal challenges to getting samples. So I conclude I don't have to."

The younger cop muttered, "She'd need a good lawyer to get away with that," but Sergeant Torres took a different approach, squatting down next to Louisa's chair so they were face-to-face.

"Mrs. Gibbs, we have no intentions of harming you. You may even need protection yourself. We need to learn all we can. Please believe that. But we have legitimate safety concerns here. We must take them seriously." She smiled. "As we also will with the letters you brought us today. But first things first. We'll get this done and it can only be helpful to you."

Louisa started to protest, and Torres quickly added, "The process should end here, OK? But it does deserve our time and attention, right?"

"It's not because his octopus organization is exerting pressure?"

Kahn stood up, looking indignant, but Torres said, "Mrs. Gibbs, come on, now. Yes, he is locally prominent, but so what? We're just trying to do our job here. If anything happened to him, and we had ignored the letters, well, then we'd sure be on the chopping block for that, wouldn't we?

"Nothing we'll do now is definitive. It will go to an expert, we'll get a report, and it will end there."

"Sure. Unless my handwriting matches these nonsense letters. I haven't even seen them. How do I know they exist?"

Torres shook her head. "We can't show them to you. That's not how a handwriting sample gets done."

Louisa looked the least little bit less like a granite statue. "Then let's get it over with. I have other things to do with my life today."

As if by magic, there was a knock on the door. A young woman came in with paper and writing instruments. She looked surprised to see extra people in the small room, but Torres assured her I would be completely quiet, a part of the furniture.

The young woman spoke to Louisa, softly but with confidence, explaining that she would do some dictating and Louisa was to write down the phrases. There would be directions to change to her other hand, to do it in block printing, and so on, but no help would be offered on spelling or placement on the page. She was to sign each page. She was to sit up straight, feet on the floor.

The soft words managed to sound very official. I would have been intimidated myself.

"I haven't taken dictation since I was a girl in French class," Louisa grumbled. "French teachers love that. We had to sit up straight then, too. That was back when dinosaurs roamed Brooklyn." But she listened, and I could see her putting some effort into it.

Were the phrases from the letters? I passed a note to Torres, who glanced at it and nodded. There were fragmentary accusations of greed and of harboring secrets. They sounded yes, very like things I had heard Louisa say. Many people had heard her say them. That wasn't good.

I would have given anything at the moment to see the whole letters.

By the time they were done, Louisa was rubbing her writing hand and her face was white with exhaustion.

"I know you are tired, so let's quickly get some questions answered about these other letters."

She asked the obvious questions, again. No post office involvement, no return address, handwritten like the letters to Towns. Always overnight. They were filled with threats disturbing yet vague. Terrible, unspecified things would happen if she did not do the right thing and promptly sell her property. That upped the ante and fit in with what I'd heard from old Mr. Prinzig. They wanted more than her garden.

The letters went on to say, cruelly, that she was old. That she no longer belonged in her home. That the world was changing and leaving her behind.

"Who belongs there more than I do, I'd like to know? You tell me that!"

The officers made no comments at all, but occasionally gave each other a meaningful look. I guessed it was along the lines of "Note this."

Finally they asked the obvious one. Did she have any idea who might be harassing her?

"You are not serious, are you? Who wants me to give up a piece of my property? Or the whole thing, it seems now? It's obvious!

They could sell their building *and* mine as a package. The buyers would tear my home down."

"But!" I had to ask. "It's landmarked. They could not touch it!"

"They'd find a way. " She looked both grim and exhausted. "They would harass and torment an old lady like me." This time I did not see any sneaky gleam in her eyes when she said "old." Did she mean it? "As they are doing now. What wouldn't they stoop to?" She closed her eyes, as if tired, but when she opened them again, she looked hard at the cops.

"I'm not folding. If I can stand up to them, you can, too!" She began gathering her things. "Now I need to leave. I have an appointment, and it is getting late."

She turned down the coffee, walked out of the office, and asked for directions to a restroom on the way. I followed her, my thoughts whirling. One of the detectives called after me, "We'll be right out. Wait for us, please."

Waiting for Louisa, I realized I was missing something. Purse, yes; car keys, no, in my jacket pocket. Jacket was back in the room we'd been in.

Chapter Six

I went back and heard Kahn saying, "How much time have we spent on this? Some nutjob acting like a schoolkid with poison-pen letters? Or two of them? And maybe a nutty old woman, too. Like we don't have any real crime to work on?"

"Why, Detective, tell me how you really feel." I could hear a little snicker. "I know, I know. But if we ignore it, and it escalates?"

"Yeah, our ass is grass. Or the boss's is."

"So we do what we must, at least go through the motions. Anyway, to make our lives complete it does seem like now we have two difficult..."

"Two nutjobs."

"Our analyst glanced at Mrs. Gibbs's letters and guessed they are not the same handwriting. Actually she said it's not even a guess, but not official until she can look deeper."

"Any chance that old broad wrote them all?"

I held my breath, listening but not believing what I heard.

"What? That's crazy."

Torres stopped, and I wondered if they were exchanging glances.

"Okay, even crazier than the fact that there are two sets of letters?"

"Seriously. Consider this. If she wrote the first ones, and thinks she's in trouble, would the second ones get her off the hook? I mean, who knows what she might think? And did you think of this? Who even writes letters anymore? Old people! People with no kind of computer. People who don't know you could use a public computer at a library."

"Are you reading detective stories again? Remember about KISS? Keep it simple, stupid? But we'll have a definitive answer on that later." Sounds of chairs scraping. "OK. Make sure she's got a way home. Maybe if you take her, she'd succumb to your charm and tell us more."

They both laughed, and I moved fast, back to the waiting area, still without my jacket. Louisa was there, and the detectives were right behind me. They had my jacket, too. We sorted out a ride for Louisa, and I waited, helping her into a cab. She looked tired and moved slowly, but was quite clear about her destination when she spoke to the driver. She was going to a building of medical offices not far from her home. Before I could ask if she needed me to come with her, she poked the driver from the back seat and said, "Make it snappy. I am late," and he took off.

Good thing too, as my car would have been left at the precinct house. Maybe I was the one who needed a keeper.

After seeing her into the car, Torres turned to me. "Who are you? You're not a relative, and you're not an employee."

When I said "How do you know?" she only smiled. She is a detective after all.

I explained how I knew Louisa, and threw in, perhaps inappropriately, that getting to know a famous figure from my college years had been an unexpected thrill.

Something sparked interest in her expression, but all she said was, "So you must know a lot about her?"

"It would depend on what you mean by 'a lot.' Why do you ask?"

"She seems like a person with an interesting past. I don't know. The whole situation is weird enough to concern me a little. Maybe she really is in some danger? Maybe Daniel Towns is? Or, maybe she is actively involved?"

"Come on!"

She looked unimpressed. "There are others who are concerned about the situation." She made a face. "It's a Class A misdemeanor. We're obligated to take a report at least." She sighed. "What happens next is not entirely my call, even if it should be." She only smiled ruefully before she left.

Was she conning me? After the overheard conversation with her colleague, it was hard to believe she was genuinely concerned. They weren't serious about any of these threats to this old woman I idolized. Their flippant attitude made me angry. I couldn't just walk away. If I could find a way to help, I would.

And then I returned to work, carrying a giant pretzel and a soda from a hot dog cart in front of the museum. Not the best lunch ever but not the worst, either.

I did my work that afternoon, but my mind was still on Louisa. I remembered seeing her on television, many years ago, talking about the destruction and neglect of city life in scorching words. And I couldn't shake thinking about her now, with her cane and her shaking hands. What else could I do?

I could talk to Dr. Kingston. He seemed to be her friend. At least I could do that. I could even call it work, because I had a new idea about that plaque. Why not discuss it in person and lead the conversation to Mrs. Gibbs?

I was in luck. He was available that evening. Hours later I waited for him at an old-school downtown Italian restaurant. No kale. No gluten-free pasta. Waiters in tuxedos. Lots of red sauce and Parm, like my elderly mother-in-law used to make. What a treat.

Glasses of wine and plates of pasta ordered, Dr. Kingston said, "So, then, you've had a new inspiration about our mystery?"

It took a second for me to remember that the first mystery we were going to discuss was not Mrs. Gibbs but the lost plaque.

"Has anyone ever tried to find the owner of the luncheonette? Did he actually go home to Nicaragua? Did he ever come back to New York? "

He smiled. "Any idea how many people named Manuel Alvarez there are out there?"

I felt myself turn red. "I see." Then I went on in a hurry. "I had something else on my mind. The plaque was kind of false pretenses. I hope you don't mind."

"I am intrigued."

I plunged in, telling him the whole story of the visit with the cops.

"Louisa is getting letters, too? That's a shock. And she never mentioned it to me." He shook his head. "Didn't want my advice, I suppose. Typical."

"What did you mean by 'too'? Did you know about Daniel Towns?"

"Oh, yes, I did. He told me himself. He is quite shaken by it. Crazy, isn't it? That there is someone with a grudge? Making accusations? Amiable Mr. Towns—and he is amiable, even when we often disagree. Hate mail!"

"But do you know what it's about? Is it personal? Or about their business, the buildings and property?"

"It does open up grounds for speculation, doesn't it?" He chuckled. "It's hard to imagine Daniel Towns has a secret life to write poison about."

"A secret life? Like…" I couldn't help it. I was at the point of giggling. "Like a drug habit? Or gambling on horse races?"

"Or a woman hidden away?" Kingston stopped, held up a hand. "The reality is that he was married, wife died years ago, no kids. Impossible to imagine him living a wild double life. This has to be about his work, but he didn't tell me any details. It's common knowledge he's in a dispute with Louisa. You know the cops want her to come in and answer questions. Isn't it obvious they would look at everyone like that?"

"Is it a crime, if it's no more than sending letters? They said a misdemeanor. What the heck does that even mean?"

"No idea. I bet it's the possibility of moving from words to action that worries them. Towns is, well, after all, he is a player in Heights business, especially now, though I'm sure he'd dispute that term." His smile was a little mocking. "His ambition is not for worldly goals, you know."

"But you know Mrs. Gibbs well, don't you? Why would someone be going after her that way?" I didn't care so much about Towns. Yes, certainly there were people who dislike his beliefs. And for him, his beliefs were his whole life. So it was not unlikely that he had some enemies.

"But she only turned to me because no one else was available." I was thinking out loud. "Would she even cooperate about Towns's letters? I don't know her well enough to ask her something like that."

"Cooperate? Louisa? Ha! Trust me, she is not used to being questioned by anyone! But you're kidding, right, asking why? You do know she's made a few enemies along the way."

"Yes. I guess I do. I'd forgotten that. But aren't they mostly businessmen? Politicians? It doesn't fit. It's so, so…"

"Childish? Yes, unless it has already escalated up to crazy." We both went silent, thinking that over.

Then he said, hesitantly, "You, that is, we, all of us who are her friends, we do have to consider something else." More hesitation. "Perhaps she actually is behind the Towns letters. The ideas sound like her, even if the sneaky method isn't her style." The sadness in his face must have mirrored my expression. "What if she is losing her grip? I know her memory is going. What if her judgment is, too? What if she even knows more about her own letters than she is telling? Think about it. How cooperative was she today?"

"She did have quite a chip on her shoulder."

"You see? Her usual combative self, or a way to deflect questions?"

"No. No, I don't believe it." I was appalled to realize my eyes were tearing up.

"Well, her friends must consider all possibilities, I believe, if we are to help her. And in spite of herself, shall we say, she does still have some friends and many, many admirers. We'll rally as much as she will allow. Help her deal with this latest two-edged worry."

"You mean, even if she doesn't appreciate it?"

We promised to keep in touch, and he said he would add me to an e-list of people who knew she needed support, even if it had to be behind her back. I had been absorbed into Friends of Louisa Gibbs. I was honored to be there.

All the way home I thought about Louisa and her friends. Who knew her well? Who could help her here? Who could I talk to without offending her? I had a hunch offending her was not difficult.

I wished the short bus ride was longer, because I didn't have a single good idea. And I wanted to talk to Joe, but I thought I shouldn't. It was someone else's life, not for idle chatter. And maybe I didn't want his advice, either.

I didn't have an idea until the next morning. And when I did, it wasn't about Louisa.

I wanted to talk to Daniel Towns again. He was the missing piece. Or, anyway, one of the missing pieces for understanding what was happening to Louisa.

I thought he must know something about those letters. That was my idea when I woke up. All I had to do was figure out how to make him want to talk to me. Not a tiny problem. First, he was a busy man. And I didn't think mentioning Louisa's name would get me very far down the track. Scratch that. It would get me way back behind the starting line.

I wondered. Theoretically I was writing something, a fascinating, timely sample chapter for the editor who had contacted me. So far this was only theoretical, but could I use it as an entry? Very politely? Just ask a few questions? And see where it could go once I had Towns's attention?

I do have a devious streak, though I try to limit it to manipulating my child as needed. After all I am an adult, not a devious teenager myself. Anymore. But this was a situation where it might work for me.

I called and spoke to an assistant. A very polite one. She agreed that Mr. Towns would be willing to talk, briefly, to a writer who was not a reporter and said she could fit me in in the early afternoon as he had another meeting canceled. He preferred face-to-face to phone. Perfect, I said.

I could take a late lunch.

I spent the morning working at my actual job, except for the moments I used to jot down my questions for Mr. Towns. My possible strategy. Yes, I was a more than a little distracted. It did occur to me that my real grown-up job was interfering with my other activities. Helping Louisa, an actual idol of mine, felt more compelling to me than my role at the museum. I firmly tamped down any consideration of what that might mean. I already had way too much to think about.

I made it to my appointment with thirty seconds to spare, no time at all to look around the vast complex where Towns's office was located. I entered the elevator from my rushed walk through the complex, adjusting my clothes, and breathing hard, trying to reach the office looking a lot more calm and composed than I felt.

His assistant spoke to him briefly and introduced me. There was not a flicker of recognition, but he welcomed me politely enough.

"I am always happy to have a chance to tell our story. What exactly did you want to know for your book?"

"Well, I am writing a chapter on Brooklyn Heights." I think I am, I thought, but did not say. "Maybe about the various subcultures like your organization, all living in this one neighborhood? The side-by-side experiences?"

"We hardly think of ourselves as a subculture." His voice was frosty.

"No, no, no. I did not meant to offend." What had I done? "Maybe community is a better word. But there are many groups, let's say, here as in any city neighborhood, and I hope to write a little about how you all have learned to live together." Had that done it?

"I see." He crossed the room to a large rack of pamphlets and selected several. "This will give you some background, how we came to be here and what our blessed goals have always been."

"Well, thank you. This will be helpful. I know you yourself have been here for a long time."

"Yes indeed, my whole adult life really. How did you know that?"

"We met, briefly, one day." I'd better be honest with him.

He looked puzzled. "Ah. Louisa Gibbs's garden. You are her friend?" Had his voice become a few degrees chillier?

"I had met her that same day. I gather there is a dispute?"

For a second he looked a lot less serene. "Yes, and our lawyers say I am not to discuss it at this time. At all. With anyone. So if that is your goal, this will be a brief conversation."

"No, no, not really. I was really wondering—" And inspiration came. "What did you think when you first came here? And where did you come from?"

"I grew up in rural Pennsylvania. Farm country. New York in the 1970s was, well…" His expression changed so rapidly I could not guess what he would say. "Oh, it was a shock. People didn't act…didn't dress… It was a shock, but not …"

"May I ask, was it confusing? I mean it was before my time, but I know, I'm a historian; it was confusing for many people."

"But I had my faith to show me the way. What more did I need?"

A light knock on the door, and the assistant came in.

"Here is the mail, Brother Towns. You said you wanted it right away. I put the important envelopes on top."

"Yes, yes, thank you, Sister Joan." Turning to me he said, "Please excuse me for a moment. We are so busy with real estate and legal matters, I must be on top of all documents whether by mail or digital." He sifted quickly through the stack, pulling out the top one and opening, nodding with satisfaction.

"That is for Sister Joan to file. The rest can wait." Then he reached the last letter and suddenly turned pale. I could see there was no stamp on the envelope. His eyes kept shifting to it as if it exerted magnetic force, all while he pretended to listen to my further questions.

Finally, I had to say it. "Please don't let me keep you from important business. I don't mind waiting while you open that." And maybe I would be able to read it upside down.

Chapter Seven

He opened it and read it while his hands trembled. His pale face grew paler, and his eyes stared vacantly, as if he were seeing something that was not his neat office and was not ordinary me. The letter fell onto his desk and then to the floor, so, naturally, I picked it up for him. I couldn't help it that my eyes glanced over it as I called for his assistant.

She hurried in, but by then he'd regained his self-control. His color had returned, and he was focusing his eyes on the letter still in my hand.

"You dropped this. I'm sorry; I didn't look at it." The appropriate white lie for the moment.

He rubbed his hand across his forehead and stared at the phone.

"I have to call the woman sergeant, don't I?" Was he addressing me or his assistant? "Torres?" He started flipping through an address book, growing frantic as he became frustrated by his inability to find the right page.

"Let me." The assistant took the book from his hands. "I'll get you her number. And a glass of water for you?"

He nodded, and she left. He stared at me.

"You did see the letter, didn't you? That vicious, lying piece of paper? I don't know what will be next. Don't know." Then he swallowed hard a few times. "You are from outside, not in our fellowship and not from the law, so maybe you have a useful, objective thought. I have never before in my whole life had a question that could not be answered by our teachings." He shook his head as if trying to clear the fog. "They keep coming and coming. And I don't understand. I don't. But you have already seen this."

He handed it back to me, and now I read it, my curiosity at war with my sympathy for this obviously frightened, elderly man. I read it a few times, and each time it seemed stranger than the last. I was relieved to see that it did not sound like Louisa, except for the anger. Biblical quotations were certainly not her style.

There were random words of hatred that sounded biblical to me. *"We were told a man or woman who is a medium or spiritist among you must be put to death."* A reference to the fire that time and what of the fire later? And to demons. Demons? Seriously? I began to feel I had gone through a looking glass into a strange world.

The perfect old-fashioned handwriting said, "*And Jesus rebuked him, and the demon came out of him, demoniacs, epileptics, paralytics; and He healed them.*" Well, that certainly sounded like the New Testament, though I had no idea where.

The last, chilling lines were, "But the fire does not purify and Jesus does not heal. Not me. Not them. That is the lie you told."

The actual sentences read like normal sentences, coherent and punctuated, but they did not make any sense.

Might there be some reality, filtered through a delusional mind, angry and wounded? What it couldn't be, I was convinced now, was anything to do with Louisa Gibbs. She'd have to have a whole second personality, which was ridiculous.

I had to say something. Anything. "I know there were other letters. Were they all like this?"

He shook his head. "At first they were only angry. Someone was angry at me. At *me*. I don't understand. And then they started talking about justice, saying I would get what I deserved. To think I have spent my whole life trying to deserve eternal blessing." He stopped, then started again, very slowly. "Trying to deserve the rewards we have been promised, but that was not what the writer meant. That much was clear." He gave me a shaky, teary smile. "The only thing that was, perhaps."

"Is it just me, or is he quoting from the Bible? Some part of the Bible?" I really wanted to know. That was certainly not Louisa's style, I thought. And hoped.

"Yes and no." He sounded a little more sure of himself. "Some are verses of the Bible, and some only have a biblical sound."

"The rhythm? Vocabulary?"

"Yes. I suppose, those things."

"The ones from before, where are they now?"

"With Miss Torres. I mean, Sergeant Torres. Evidence, she said."

Like Louisa's. That made sense, but I was disappointed.

"But I have copies."

"I should have guessed. Could I see them?"

"Yes, yes, why not? I have already said more than the good sergeant would like, and shared outside the fellowship more than I ever should have."

There they were, five letters in all, handwritten the old-fashioned way, like the newest one. Nothing to create a disguise, like cut-out and pasted letters or a word-processed page. Or even a typewriter. Not a very smart harasser, I thought, and immediately wondered what the police might have learned.

The letters did escalate, from somewhat mild comments about hypocrisy to the loony ravings I had just read. The earliest actually could have been something Louisa might say, though it was impossible to imagine her slipping out late at night to drop off secret mail. The later letters could not possibly be from her.

"Did you know Louisa Gibbs is also getting threatening letters?" I said it softly, no accusation, but I watched him carefully.

"Louisa?"

Was that an almost smile? It quickly changed into a face of serious concern, the frank open look he usually wore.

"That is very strange, isn't it? Someone harassing Louisa? Though she certainly has made enemies over the years. I myself..." He stopped, tapped the desk with his fingers, looked away from me. "We have had our difficult moments over the years, when appropriate manners and, um, respect, were worn very thin. A scary woman, to be sure." He looked back at me, less frightened now and more curious. "What did they say?"

"I have not seen them." An easy out and conveniently the truth.

"But the authorities have? That sergeant woman?"

I nodded.

"Well, that is good. I don't wish her any harm. If only she would come to her senses, we could be cordial neighbors, I'm sure. "

"You won't be a neighbor for long, right? Maybe none of this matters?"

"In a sense, none of it does. Very true." He looked calmer now, less disturbed. "Still, I will have to contact NYPD about this new letter. And offer any assistance for Louisa's situation, too. We must render unto Caesar."

He stood up, once more the chubby old man with an air of authority oddly mixed with humility. "Sister Joan, I'll take that police phone number now. And you should walk Ms. Donato to the elevator, please."

She came in with a pillbox and counted out three multicolored tablets, scolding him softly for forgetting. She poured a glass of water and said, "I'll wait while you swallow them."

Then I was quite firmly dismissed. The young lady whispered as we walked, "He scared me there for a few minutes. He was so stressed, and he isn't well."

"I noticed you brought him some medication?"

"He isn't reliable about taking it. Sometimes he forgets."

"You seem almost as upset as he was."

"I worry. He's such a good man, he is so devoted to his work and our beliefs, and he's dedicated his whole life. But this huge task, getting all the sales completed, is wearing him out. I'm not the only one worried about him, of course." She looked at me seriously. "He's so valued and beloved here. So we try to take good care of him." The elevator bumped.

"And here we are. Come on. The exit door is right around here. And then here."

She guided me expertly through the corridors and said goodbye. "You'll find the gate easily if you keep to the right past the next two buildings. Got that?"

I was back in the rest of the world in a few minutes. It was a long walk up the hill that gave the Heights its name, to where I would find transportation back to work. I had to stop and get my breath at one of the benches along Louisa's street.

I saw Nancy Long down the street, leaning against a fence. She was watching the scene on the street. Just watching.

An instant detour for me.

"Hello, Nancy. How are you? I'm Erica. Joe introduced us a few days ago?"

She nodded. "Yes. At that dreadful party. I hate those kind of people." She didn't turn to look at me. She stared across the street and did not say another word.

It's hard to have a conversation with someone who does not want to converse back, but I was determined to try. I leaned against the fence, too.

"Didn't you say you do work for Louisa Gibbs? I know her a little. How is she doing?"

"I've been at her house today." I stared, and she finally turned to me. "She'd be doing okay, if only they'd leave her alone. Mind their own business. And yet they go on and on, just to make a little more on their property." She looked away. "Sorry. I don't have good memories of that world." She turned a little pink, as if embarrassed to have said that much, and would not meet my eyes.

"What do you mean? Are you...?"

"Was. I was. This is not a secret. Joe knows, so I figured you must have heard. I don't talk about it, though. Let the past bury itself is my first commandment."

"But! But how did you stand working for Louisa all these years?" I just blurted it out. "Right next door to one of their buildings? You said that, didn't you?" I was sure I remembered it. "That you work for her in spite of the neighbors?"

"Why not?" The stare she gave me was almost as hostile as her words. "Why should I let them take any more away from me? I like her. And her house! How could I resist an old beauty like that?" She said it with a face of stone. "How I do it? I try to pretend they are not there."

"How's that working for you?"

She did finally look at me then. "Lately, not so great."

"You mean because of Louisa's dispute with them?"

"Well, sure. We've grown close, her and me. I, well, I don't have any family. Not now. And hers are all gone. And she was one of my first little jobs, way before they put up that monster."

There were more stories here for sure. Maybe not part of my work, but even if not, I wanted to know more.

"But now? It's gotten hard, with them really harassing her."

I was taking a chance when I responded, "They would say she is harassing them."

"That's what they always say." Her voice was as hard as her face. "Sometimes it's even true. There is a long history of that. You could find out. But hell. Sometimes it's a damn excuse to do whatever they want." She stopped. "And wouldn't they be shocked if they heard me using those words? But they'd hear only if they spoke to me. Which they don't."

She pointed across the street. "See him?" It was Daniel Towns, emerging from a car and walking into their building. "Known him since I was kid. He walks right past me if we happen to meet on the street." Her voice changed. "These people honor me with their lips, but their hearts are far from me." She gave me another hard look. "That's Mark 7:6, riffing on Isaiah. An admonishment they conveniently forget."

"Towns? Is he really that bad? I just talked to him today. He seems to be a hardworking, worried, mild sort of old guy. And stressed about his responsibilities right now."

"Well, you bought his act." She wouldn't look at me. "He is also hard-hearted and hardheaded, like all the leaders. Only one way is right, and it's for sure his. Life on the straight and narrow path. No room for anyone who wants some curves." Her expression grew harder with each word. "He's worried and stressed? Well, boo-hoo."

She stood and picked up her bags. "I must be going. Places to be. So long." She stopped for a tiny second and whispered, "No one deserves stress more than Daniel Towns. Or pain. Or guilt."

I walked back to the subway and returned to my office with my head spinning. This lunchtime excursion had turned out to be far more confusing than I had expected. I wondered and wondered how much Nancy Long really hated Daniel Towns. Was it more than talk to her?

In my first free minute I called the one person who might actually know something solid. Sergeant Torres was available. In fact she answered the phone herself.

"It's Dr. Donato. We met when I accompanied Louisa Gibbs to the precinct."

"Yes, I remember. What can I do for you?"

I told her about my experience with Daniel Towns and my conversation with Nancy Long. She noted the latter and said about Towns, "He's already contacted us. Naturally, we continue to be concerned."

"Concerned? Would I be out of line to ask what that actually means? In plain Brooklyn English?"

"I figured you for a Brooklyn girl." I could hear a smile in her voice. "I've wanted to talk to you anyway. You mentioned you researched and wrote about earlier days in Brooklyn Heights, and I asked around about you. We could use some more help on that."

What could I do but say, "Tell me more."

"Can you meet with me? This is a little, um, let's say it's confidential. "

I could and I would. No way would I resist that invitation.

"You remember where we are, on Gold Street?"

That was in the labyrinth of crowded, low-end commercial streets of downtown Brooklyn, near the entrance to the expressway.

"Yes."

She named a nearby bar, not a cop hangout. "Private, and obscure. You know?"

I did know the street. I'd find it. Tonight? I agreed, left messages for Joe and Chris. I had a tiny pang about Joe, but I got over it. And Chris often foraged her own dinner even when I was home. This was too strange, really, for me to pass up. And I wanted to put in a good word for Louisa.

Torres was in the back corner of a corner booth, the most obscure seat in the place, back to the wall, eyes front. She looked as drab as before. A not-uniform uniform, I thought. I sat down, ordered a beer, glanced at the menu.

"I wouldn't stray from the bar snacks. They don't exactly cook here." She flashed an unexpected smile.

I looked around at the greasy, yellowed walls and chipped tile floor and said, "I've been in places like this before. I'll stick to French fries, right?"

Looking serious and even stressed, she laid it out for me. "We could use better information about the feud between the Watchtower Society and Louisa Gibbs. It looks like it might be related to all this mess."

I was surprised.

"I'll try to explain what I know. It's not much." And I did, ending with, "How is this helpful?"

Torres made a face and only answered, "I can't tell you, but you can think it through. And to make our lives complete, we were under some pressure about the ongoing disagreements even before those letters and all, even though it's actually a civil matter."

"I don't understand at all."

She sighed. "Politics. Politicians. Can't get away from them. These real estate deals involve lots of money, lots of big shots." She morosely sipped her drink. "In their own eyes, anyway, if not in ours. But it will be our asses if this escalates, that is for sure."

"But I still don't see where I come in."

"We need to know more about Daniel Towns and about Louisa Gibbs. We've already checked public records. No arrests, no lawsuits, no legal issues of any kind."

"Which surprised…?"

"Right. Exactly no one. Both upright citizens all the way. But someone out there—someone!—doesn't see it that way. Or maybe two someones. Which brings us to those letters."

"But it all seems so incongruous. Like, hate mail is so…?"

"Junior high?" She almost, almost smiled. "So I had this idea. What if we go back further? Maybe we'll come up with something to question or something that helps us make sense of it. What if we're missing something from the past?"

I almost laughed. "I just had this conversation with Dr. Kingston. We were discussing the threatening letters."

I could see her frown even in the dim light of the bar.

"What are you talking about?" She took a deep breath before she said any more. "You agreed not to talk about it when you came in the other day."

"I didn't. *He* told *me*." I was surprised she was surprised and told her what I knew.

"Damn. Damn! Someone's been gossiping. Honestly, a cop house is as bad as a hen house. Gabble, gabble, gabble." I guessed someone's head would roll for this. She looked grim. "OK. The problem is I don't have anyone who has the time to dig deep.

We've got a few other *actual* crimes to deal with! I'm thinking maybe someone like you would have more expertise in that kind of digging anyway. Ya know?"

"I could look around. I mean, I know some sources, sure. But it could take a while, and it's a crapshoot. I can't promise any results. Plus, I have a job, responsibilities. I don't know how I would squeeze it in." But my mind was racing. I would definitely find a way to squeeze it in. Of course I would.

She leaned back, considering. "I'm wondering if you would be more susceptible to pleas of civic duty or offers of money."

"Try both." I had to laugh, and she even laughed with me.

"Ha. So, don't you feel you have a responsibility to help solve this problem? Keep the wheels of the community turning smoothly?" She stared into my eyes, checking to see if she was getting anywhere. Then she added "Also, I do have some funds for confidential informants. How'd you like to become one?"

I briefly flashed on my father's expression if I told him that. Or Joe. I flashed on what they were sure to say, too. And they wouldn't be wrong either. Or not exactly wrong.

She looked at me and smiled. "You know you want to."

She got that right, but I said, cautiously, "Can I have overnight to think about it?"

"Fair enough. Give me a ring in the morning, OK?" She sounded confident. "By the way, we know now Mrs. Gibbs didn't write those letters to Towns. Handwriting wasn't a match. No idea who did. Not yet," she added. "We will."

"And what about the ones she got?"

"They are still working on those. The same person did not write both sets of letters." She saw my surprised face and smiled. "I know. That would have made it easier."

She seemed to decide something. "The experts think the Towns letters are someone imitating Mrs. Gibbs's handwriting."

"What? No way. Why in the world? How could they come up with that?"

"No idea. But the why might be..."

"I see. Someone trying to get her in trouble?"

"Could be. And I wonder why I have a headache every day! You want to take a look? At both sets? Just to see what they said? Might be that I could arrange that."

"You know I do." I added, "Do you ever go fishing?"

She was startled, then she did smile, almost a full grin. "I grew up in Sheepshead Bay. Fishing boats all over. I know how to hook them, yes, I do."

"I give in. I'm hooked." I held my hands up in surrender. "I will help you. What do you need me to do?"

"Find out what you can about Gibbs, the property itself, and Towns, as far back as you can go. Everything. Our citizens at the Watchtower Society are not exactly being forthcoming. They feel like we have no right to look at the old records. They are claiming some are missing, destroyed in a flood, blah, blah, blah. Stalling us."

"I don't get it. Don't they want to protect Mr. Towns?"

"They do. And they don't. Ya know? They are a closemouthed bunch."

I still wasn't quite done with the complications.

"One last thing. Tell me the truth, if you can."

Torres raised her eyebrows at that, but she listened.

"How can you possibly believe Louisa Gibbs is involved in any of this? This craziness? Anything criminal? When she spent her whole life working for the public good?"

"Others might disagree with that."

"All right, all right. *Her* belief about the public good, OK? And no one who knows her would think for a minute she is mentally incapable."

She looked away from me for a long moment. Finally, she nodded, as if making a decision. "Yes. Yes, it seems out of character. That's what anyone would think. But you must know this—we are obligated to look at everything and everyone. Yes, it seems the handwriting issue on those letters is resolved, though it doesn't prove she was not involved in the threats some other way. No, don't bother to argue. It sounds too much like her to convince everyone that she is in the clear." She stopped again, sipped her beer, sighed. "Anyone who is not you, anyway."

She swallowed the last of her drink. "Obviously, we are digging deeper into it. Think about it as you look at your information and remember your view might not be the whole one? Yes?"

I agreed to that caveat. I sure didn't want to, but what choice was there?

Chapter Eight

"I know we don't have sleepovers on school nights, but, Mom! We have a yearbook meeting before classes. Really, really early, and Mel's dad said he'd drive us."

That's how the next day began. She wanted to spend the night at her best friend Mel's. I wanted to stick to my rules.

"You know this makes sense. Are you afraid we're up to something? Going clubbing?" She saw my hesitation. Maybe I did think something like that? Or worry about it, anyway? "Seriously? Would you talk to Mel's mom already?"

So I did, and the plan as presented was true. Parents would be home. Girls would go to school early. What could I do but say yes? I didn't want to be unreasonable. I encouraged working on yearbook. I didn't want my daughter to think I didn't trust her. Even though I didn't. I remembered my own teen years too well.

And Joe would be home from his job out on the shore. Okay, call me stupid that I didn't think about that earlier.

I casually wandered upstairs and casually stood in her doorway, watching as she collected her overnight things.

"Joe is back tonight. You won't get to see him when he gets here."

Her back to me, intensely examining a nightshirt for her bag, she mumbled, "I'll see him soon enough." That's when I knew this was a setup, part of Chris's long campaign to play Cupid. It had intensified some, now that she had a boyfriend of her own.

I wanted to hug her, but I could see she wanted to believe her little plan had worked. And later, it did work.

He came home to a table set for dinner, wineglasses out, candles lit, purchased sushi decoratively arranged on a platter. A little celebration. We were so glad to see each other, I didn't even worry about what it meant. About how deep a part of each other's lives we had become.

We woke early and made good use of the time, then it was suddenly late, and I dashed out to work. Lucky Joe, who worked for himself. No one would question if he showed up late on a visit to a house in renovation; they'd assume he was delayed at another house. And so he was. At mine.

I slid into my office chair, hoping no one had seen me, switched my computer on, and there it was, a completely forgotten deadline.

Good morning to me. My first email was a reminder that I owed someone a blog post. Who they heck were they? The media outreach team, the one charged with raising the museum profile among media-savvy art lovers. Young ones mostly. Modern museum marketing. Every department had a designated schedule to write something interesting—no, fascinating. Or charming. And recent. Something about behind the scenes. With photos. To add relatability. What a stupid word that was.

I swore. It was my turn and I had completely forgotten about it. Due tomorrow. This was like being back in school, struggling to keep on top of deadlines. I did not need this today.

It didn't have to be long. It didn't have to—in fact shouldn't be—scholarly. It merely had to be there, sent in by tomorrow morning.

I thought frantically about what I'd been doing. The architectural sculpture project could be written about eventually—even in my panic, I could see that—but it was too big for five hundred words. And we were still right in the middle of it. I would suggest it for a longer piece. Some other time.

"First impressions of a new employee?" Boring. And who would care? "Exploring Brooklyn Heights?" Certainly not. Not part of the Museum message, content, responsibilities. In fact the less I said about what I'd been doing lately, the better. "Observations of a working mother in the Museum." Very boring, and surely been done before. I had nothing earthshaking to say, at least not yet. "Were they doing a good job of attracting teens?" I had the teen but I hadn't been here long enough to know the answer. (I would look into it when I had time. Interview Chris and her friends? And how much would I embarrass my daughter if I did? And was that a plus or a minus?)

I needed to stop thinking so much.

There on my desk was the folder on the Whitman plaque. Hmm. A mystery, always intriguing. Relevant to the museum? Absolutely. Coverable in the space provided? Sure.

I could write it up in an hour, but it would still need some photos. I had the very old one of the plaque itself. Perfect. Research here might turn up one of the old building. I should add one of the modern location where it used to be. Show what replaced it? Maybe, as a classy touch, a Whitman quote from the engraved fence at Empire Fulton Ferry Park.

I was on a roll. A quick check of my calendar showed nothing for this afternoon. I could be there and back in a short time, if I could avoid being sidetracked. No dropping in on Louisa today. I was on a mission.

I wrote the blog first draft in record time. Instead of wasting time trying to figure out how to scan in the photos I had, I found a tech-savvy intern to do it. I was finally getting smarter about being a little further up the ladder.

Then, once again, I was on my way back to Brooklyn Heights.

I trudged down the hill from the subway to the Empire Fulton Ferry part of Brooklyn Bridge Park and used my phone to take some quick photos. They wouldn't be good, but I was confident that the media team could use their magic to fix them up.

I trudged back up the hill to what is now Cadman Plaza, an enclave of middle-income apartment towers mixed with low-rise town houses, carved out of a high-traffic area. An interior path was quaintly called Pineapple Walk. Nicely planted too. It was attractive, I had to admit.

Cadman Plaza was a fancier name for what used to be Cranberry Street at the corner of Fulton; the lost plaque had hung there, on the actual building where the Rome Brothers Print Shop once occupied space.

My concentration on framing a photo that would be evocative was ripped apart by a siren. Police? Ambulance? It was always a threatening sound, but things happened here. This was adjacent to a busy street lined with courthouses and feeding into the Brooklyn Bridge. I ignored it.

Then a fire truck came screaming past me, and another was down the street. I looked up, looked around, and saw clouds of smoke coming from somewhere toward the river. Deep in the residential part of Brooklyn Heights.

This was not the ordinary sound of big-city traffic. I stashed my phone and walked toward the smoke at a smart pace, silently cursing the many streetlights that forced me to stop on the way.

By the time I was getting close enough to work out where the smoke was coming from, real fear was attacking, the kind that makes swallowing hard and rushing necessary. It was Louisa's beautiful street. Another block and I turned a corner to see the street closed, fire trucks on the block, a scene of great confusion. Firefighters with huge hoses and scary-looking tools were moving with great purpose toward—yes. Louisa's house and the building next door, the Witnesses' dorm.

People were still pouring out of the dorm, with firefighters yelling into bullhorns, herding them across the street. There was an ambulance, too. Had anyone been hurt? Anyone I knew? Who could I ask?

Where was Louisa? She should be in the crowd crossing the street, with her neighbors, the Witnesses. I could see the firefighters circling her house, too, carrying equipment and gathering on the porch, but I could not get close. There were barriers blocking off the street. Large men, too.

Television news reporters, loaded with portable equipment, were roaming around, apparently getting in the way, but asking the questions I wanted to ask. I slithered as close as I could get, but I couldn't get close enough, so I melted back into the crowds, keeping my eyes open for any familiar face.

An EMS worker walked by, and I jumped into her path to ask about the ambulance.

"No, no," she answered, barely stopping. "We are only standing by now, just in case. We took two people to the ER to be checked out, but that's all."

And was Louisa, in front of her door, having a heated discussion with men who had axes? I pushed through to the barrier in time to catch the words "irreplaceable" and "treasured." Finally she stepped back and allowed them in. One of them turned and escorted her across the street, where I lost sight of her in the crowd.

A suffocating, noxious smell filled the air. I felt myself choking, coughed, and scrabbled around in my purse for a candy. Someone stopped in front of me.

"Dr. Donato? Do you need help?"

It was Sierra, the hipster girl who worked for Louisa.

'No, no," I gasped. "But you? Do you know…?"

She handed me her water bottle, and a long swig helped me recover.

"Do you know what happened? Have you talked to Mrs. Gibbs?"

"Hell no. I was going to ask you. I've been so afraid of something like this. I remind her all the time to only smoke outside and with her ashtray in her hand, and she doesn't like that, not one bit."

The circling firemen had gone into Louisa's house, but I couldn't see what they were doing from the outside.

"Was it a cigarette? Does anyone know?"

"I don't know. They're telling us nothing. Jerks! When I got here, there were flames on both sides of her fence and in the garden. Oh, she will be so upset."

Firefighters were spraying their giant python-like hoses on the fence between the two properties and in Louisa's beloved garden. And smoke was still rising at the foundations of both buildings.

"I did see her talking to the firefighters, but then she disappeared in the crowd. She might need some help."

"Yes, yes, I'm trying. This is so scary and she is, you know, not well." She rubbed away the tears rolling down her face. "It's the damn smoke fumes. But I am so worried. She's not answering her cell phone. Probably left it in the house."

And then, there she was, standing up with an impeccably camera-ready reporter, looking tousled and fragile herself, but sounding like, well, like Louisa. I grabbed Sierra and pointed.

Louisa looked exhausted but stood straight and spoke firmly. "My house will stand, as it has for a large part of Brooklyn's life. There is smoke damage." She waved her hand dismissively. "It can be repaired and cleaned."

The reporter asked, "How do you think it got started? Electrical failure?"

She gave the interviewer a look that could have singed an oak tree. "I had all the wiring updated to code some years ago. And, yes, I do smoke, but I am careful. It did not start in my home, but outdoors. I am sure of it. Sure! The fencing right over there has the most damage. There is a crime here, and I have complete faith that our city's investigators will figure it out. It's sheer luck no one was killed. Whoever did this is a potential murderer."

Her jaw set, as if she were stopping herself from saying any more, but her eyes flickered to the building next door. The reporter thanked her and went to break.

I could hardly believe it. A woman of her age, after a terrifying experience, and she was up and out and ready to get into another battle.

Sierra and I linked arms and pushed our way through, while Louisa didn't notice us as she talked to another reporter. We waited, impatiently, until she was free.

"Erica! And Sierra! I'm so glad to see you. Isn't this terrible?"

I was surprised at how enthusiastic she sounded.

"Did you hear me being interviewed? That'll show them, won't it?"

"What?" I was more than a bit confused. "What will it show them? And who will it show?"

"That I am not a confused old woman to be pushed around. There it is, right on television tape for the whole world to see, right? And that I know what they did."

All right. She was thinking two moves ahead as always. Or so I'd been told about her in her glory days. I could see that asking how she was would be a waste of time.

"What is it you are thinking?"

"Isn't it obvious? Someone set that fire! And I know who my enemy is these days. They wanted to scare me into becoming an old lady who will say yes to anything. "

I thought, "Fat chance," but I said, "How is the house? Has anyone told you anything at all?"

"Not yet. They're still checking for safety, but they sort of said unofficially, it seems like only smoke and some water damage outside. The building held. They knew how to build them in those days. I've already asked Nancy to take a look, as soon as the fire department will let her. I suppose there will be lots of delays with insurance and so on. On and on, I suspect, but she promised to do the work right away.

"Now, my dears, here is someone else to interview me. Sierra, I'll call tonight to let you know about work." She turned away, almost smiling. "I seem to be a public figure again."

I went home laughing to myself. The crisis had done the exact opposite of what I expected. She was energized instead of crushed.

Joe's reaction, when I told him about my day, was different. I'd intended to ask him what he knew about fires in old houses, but the conversation was sidetracked from the start.

"How deep are you getting pulled into this conflict? And into this woman's life?"

"Exactly what do you mean by that?"

"You know you have a history of getting sucked into situations a long way from your work or life?"

I didn't agree. He wasn't exactly wrong, but damned if I was telling him he was right.

"So you have a new job to keep you busy and a family life, but I see you obsessing about a conflict that has nothing to do with either. You can write a different article! And if she is right, that this was deliberate, what are you walking into?"

Seeing my stubborn face, he unwisely added, "Come on! It's already ugly. What if it gets dangerous?"

"I don't believe this!" I jumped up and started clearing the table of the dishes still holding our dinner. "You sound like my father! And you know how I feel about him when he starts that!"

He looked at me quizzically, and his voice was so carefully reasonable, I was offended. "You know he isn't wrong all the time. Maybe this would be one of them?"

I sat down again, arms folded, face grim. I could l feel it in the set of my jaw.

"At my age he does not get to tell me what to do *or* what not to do. And you are not even my father."

"So what am I? I'm only trying to be the man taking care of you." He smiled, and that was the last straw for me. I got up again, and walked out, throwing back over my shoulder, "Right now, you are the man who is annoying me beyond words. And I am not your rescue pet to take care of."

I stamped upstairs, noisily, and it didn't hit me until later that my pounding steps were just like Chris's when she was having a hissy fit. And I knew I was too old for that, especially right after proclaiming I was too mature to be bossed around.

Those thoughts came later, after I had been lying on my bed, head under a pillow, for some time. I heard Joe leave. It's a small house. The sound of the front door slamming traveled right up the stairs.

Later I heard Chris come home and knock on my door, and I called out, "Go away! I need alone time!"

She didn't say a word.

I think I fell asleep, because in the next moment the room was dark and I knew I had to apologize. My least favorite interaction. Joe was not downstairs, and Chris had her door closed with music on, wisely distancing herself from adult emotion. It wouldn't get easier if I waited, and now I wanted him to come home. Right now.

It was a while, long enough for me to imagine the worst. That he'd never come back? That my temper had ruined what we had? Which was pretty great, whatever it was. Had he called an ex-girlfriend? There was that tall redhead who'd never quite given up.

Chapter Nine

He walked in right after I poured a glass of wine. I didn't say a word. I just poured one for him. He drank it while he paced my living room. My living room is too small for effective pacing. It would have been funny, in other circumstances. Not now.

When he finally stopped, he stood at the other side of the room, arms crossed, frowning, and said, "So I worry about you. How is that wrong?"

I whispered, "It isn't."

The frown smoothed out a little.

"Then what the hell was that all about?"

"Because...because...I still need to make my own decisions about what I do. You know? Mom and Dad got me through the worst time of my life, but then they didn't know how to stop. Now I'm used to being on my own, and..." I stopped. I didn't know where I wanted to go from there, but Joe almost smiled.

"Sounds like..." He paced some more. "Maybe we need to get used to being in a relationship? Both of us? How long has it been?"

I shook my head. "Since Jeff died?" I had tears in my eyes. "Maybe never. Not really. Just passing connections. Nothing real."

By then he was on my side of the room, hands on my shoulders. "And you know my life. You were a friend for some of it. After getting divorced, I spent my time on fun and games. No regrets and no hard feelings."

I started to smile myself. He pulled me close. Apparently we were done fighting, at least for now. Being in a relationship was turning out to be more complicated than I expected, but for now, this was enough.

The next morning, Saturday, I was humming in the kitchen as I started the coffee. It was so late, even teen vampire Chris sleepily wandered into the kitchen and cautiously eyed me up and down.

"I see the storm is over. You are humming. And playing homemaker." She flashed me a smart-aleck grin, and I was happy enough to do no more than flick a dish towel at her.

I skipped the possible smart-aleck response.

"Any chance of pancakes, since you seem to be in the mood?"

"Already started. Get the syrup."

Joe followed soon after, appallingly wide awake and ready to discuss the day. The maple syrup was almost gone, which suggested a visit to the vast local farmers' market—we call them Greenmarkets in New York—for syrup, fall apples, and perhaps a pie. Chris put in a bid for apple-walnut pie and some of those tiny rolls from the baker. "Lots of tiny rolls. I like the ones with seeds. And the ones with cranberries."

Now that we were friends again, I asked Joe what he knew about old houses and fire safety. His answer was that if it was Nancy who updated Louisa's house, it was done right. He put his money on arson, and I didn't even take the bet.

The market, right at the grand plaza in front of the park entrance, was crowded with dogs and their owners coming from walks, bikers coming from rides, and baby strollers. Many languages and many accents. City life at its best. And still it turned out to be surprising how romantic produce shopping on a bright fall day could be. We shared a cherry pie for lunch and buried the evidence where Chris would not find it.

And when I could, I sneaked a peek at news sources, hoping to find an update about the fire, but there was nothing out there yet, only some stories saying there was no news but that the source was keeping an eye on it. Could they be any more unhelpful?

Next day, deep in my work, puzzling out the implications of a memo about the division of research responsibilities, I had an unexpected text. It was from Fitz. Fitz? Oh, Fitz. That book editor. He attached a newspaper article about the fire. Did he think I wouldn't have heard about it? As if.

I'd had nagging advisers for my dissertation. I had spent a lot of years writing it. I was careful, scholarly, fact driven, and analytical. Fitz's ideas about stories of living in changing Brooklyn were quite different.

Or alternately, he had no ideas at all, just a collection of glib phrases. "*Très* Brooklyn" was the most ridiculous, but he swore it meant a lot.

He asked when he could see those sample chapters. I wrote back, "When I can." I stopped myself from writing "Maybe never." Even more, I wanted to write, "Ha-ha." I had no idea what I was going to do.

When I was back home that evening, my dad showed up to watch a game with Joe. No one had told me about this, but I decided to be mature and not object. They were absorbed, so I didn't even bother arguing with my dad about anything. We were both trying, but we tended to rub each other the wrong way. And no one had better say in my hearing that it was because we were too similar.

Anyway, what I wanted was to explore fire investigation. How long would it take to have answers about the fire? Who was investigating, police or fire? Or maybe both? Sergeant Torres might know. Would know, probably. Geographically, her turf, I thought.

However, what I needed to do was work for my actual paying NYPD job. No research I had done earlier was useful at all, even though Brooklyn Heights was red-hot real estate, with every detail and rumor closely followed by local sources. Searching online, no matter how I did it, just produced too much to wade through, all well-known and none of it useful to me.

I left to go to the Brooklyn history division of the library and dig through the clipping files. I called to the menfolk over the loud broadcast—why are sports programs so noisy?—and left to get some work done. The afternoon was disappearing too rapidly.

Find random useful information about Louisa, as I had begun to think of her, and the Watchtower Society and Brooklyn Heights. I needed information not in the easy public records. Yes, there were tons of information that mentioned both parties, but nothing that told me anything new. But, I thought, she had lived a public life. There must be more.

At first I found nothing I had not seen before. This call for historic protection, that concern over inappropriate historic reconstruction of old buildings, with them on opposite sides, and long since resolved. Nervous residents talking about the ongoing sale of the Witnesses buildings and what it meant. All very public, all very known by those who were interested, and sometimes hotly disputed, but nothing close to what I was looking for.

I began again, anxiously checking the clock for the room's closing hours. I looked this time very specifically at Louisa's own home and the more modern Watchtower-built structure next to it. I tried not to become sidetracked by the oldest photos, showing the famous Gibbs mansion when it was new and a valued addition to the Brooklyn Heights streetscape.

The exterior had changed only a little over time. Some minor changes made it more fashionable as tastes changed. In the society pages I found family portraits from the 1920s, as they hosted large Christmas parties. There were gigantic evergreens in the drawing room where we had tea. They were decorated with real candles, and a dressed-up family stood in front of it, a woman in a beaded 1920s chemise dress, a man and some boys in high-collared dress shirts and three-piece suits, like actors in silent films. The man had a watch chain draped across his elegant vest. And there was a tiny girl with a Dutch bob, a giant bow in her hair, and a belligerent expression. Louisa. She had the same fierce gaze she had now.

Buried in there was a subfile, perhaps misfiled decades ago. It was clippings about a fire on that block.

That got my attention. The old houses often did not have good fireproofing, or any at all. Some were wood, not stone, and some stone ones had old wood frameworks that caught fire easily and burned quickly. There was a famous wintertime fire that destroyed a hotel because the cold froze the water lines. I had seen photos of the fire trucks covered with ice.

This one was in 1973, and it destroyed a building at what was—wait a minute, I thought. Did I have the address correct? I found a photo. Yes. The fire destroyed the old building next to Louisa's house, the one on the spot where the Watchtower building now stood. And hadn't Mr. Towns told me that it was a derelict building, demolished for the new construction? Impossible that he had not known about the dramatic fire. Something was weird about this.

I took the time to read it all. This was a very old building, dry as tinder, with apartments above and the first floor long ago turned into small shops.

It was the last article, which I skimmed quickly in the flickering lights signaling closing time, that riveted my complete attention. A week after that fire, it was established that there were three deaths. One elderly tenant who had not heard the alarms and trucks, and two workers in the shop.

And then I read that the shop on the ground floor, completely destroyed, was a witchcraft store. How was that possible? I had to go back and read it again. And then one more time. I kept thinking that was impossible. I must have misunderstood.

The library was closing as I read the article. No time even to make a copy of it, with a security officer walking through, clearing the room, so I noted the source—the old-fashioned way, with pen and paper—and went down the stairs and through the atrium with the other stragglers, still dumbfounded by what I had read.

No historical imagination could put such a shop on that quietly genteel street. Mine couldn't. I tried all the way home, and my highly trained historical imagination is more powerful than most.

I wanted to look for more, but life engulfed me as soon as I went through the door. Chris needed help with an assignment and a chance to complain about her unrelenting teachers. My help was forthcoming; my sympathy was limited.

Game over, Dad was gone and Joe had a big welcome hug and dinner still warm on the stove. I put my work in the mental compartment where it belonged and took out my other self, but late at night, in my dark, quiet house, I was suddenly wide awake. I had taken on a job and so far had produced nothing useful. Or was what I had stumbled on today useful? If not, would I still be paid for my time? Typical 3:00 a.m. thoughts suited to that dark, quiet time when anxiety attacks.

The true solution was to stop squeezing my eyes shut in the vain hope that doing so would force me back to sleep and get up to do something. It would involve a computer and more research in my silent house.

I found the article I'd seen in the library folder and typed in the name of the shop. There it was, a very old photo, older than I am, a streetscape with the store's facade. Wise Women Krafte. An old building, not quaint, not elegant, in fact barely livable, right next to Louisa's elegant home. I thought about the bizarre neighbor interactions it must have created. So. Proof that I had not imagined the whole thing. Now I was wide awake

And were there stories. Most were fascinating, absurd, nostalgic, and highly suspect as history, written by people who had sampled the witchcraft scene of the time. Yes, to my astonishment, there really was such a scene, complete with self-designated witches. And it was not in a dark German forest or an ancient Celtic hilltop but right here in Brooklyn. Before I was even born, there they were amid the striving young families who were starting up nursery schools and renovating brownstones with sweat equity. There amid the clean-cut, clean-shaven, clean-thinking, fresh-from-small-town-America Jehovah's Witnesses. There amid the fashionable young people in their flowered, baggy shirts, long hair, miniskirts, all the swirling Day-Glo of a Peter Max poster. And recreational drugs. The lyrics of "White Rabbit" were quoted often: "Feed your head!" Articles took it for granted there was some overlap between psychedelic styles, psychedelic substances, and the mysticism of the other realms.

As my head was drooping toward my keyboard, I went back to bed, to a confusing sleep full of bright paisley swirls of color that became progressively darker, and a kind of droning music. Sitar? Lovely at first, then hypnotic. And then, disturbing.

It was a relief to wake up to my everyday world of chilly fall rain, coffee and toast, Joe singing in the shower, Chris's after-school agenda. It pushed away those disturbing dreams in an instant.

At work I wrote a mundane report, lunched with a friendly colleague, avoided a supercilious one. OK'd Chris's text about after-school plans. Sent a smiley face emoji in response to Joe's "Spaghetti tonight?" And still heard the drone of that sitar in my mind.

And then I got the first letter. When I came home, it lay on the floor of my foyer, in between the outer and inner door, under the mail slot, mixed in the pile of junk mail and worthy and unworthy requests for money. As if I had a cent to spare. No stamp. No postmark. A thick luxurious envelope with my name in ink, elegantly handwritten. It looked like a wedding invitation. Odd, I thought. I wasn't expecting any special events. It said, "Stop looking at matters that don't concern you. Consider this a warning."

I dropped it as if it burned my hand, and then picked it up again. If the sender wanted to get my attention, he—she? they?—had succeeded. Then I set it aside. Then I picked it up again and put it in my desk drawer. I did not want Chris to see it lying around. I did not want Joe to see it, and…hmm. Because I did not want to have the discussion that would follow? Not yet. I didn't think it out very thoroughly. Possibly I thought if I could hide it and not tell anyone, it would disappear.

That didn't work at all. There was another envelope the next day. This time it said, "Pay attention. We are watching. We know."

That scared me, even while a voice in my mind said, "This is all bravado." What could they be watching? And what could they know? Whoever it is.

But the smarter part of my mind reached for the phone and called Sergeant Torres.

When I told her, there was a long silence before she said "That's not good." Then there were the questions. Any vandalism? Face-to-face threats? Or by phone or social media? Had I been followed? By car or on foot?

I had a clear no to most of them. The one about being followed had to be "Not that I know of."

Another long silence, then, "You're not qualified to give a definitive answer, but what is your overall impression? Does it look at all like the handwriting of the ones Towns was getting? Or Gibbs?"

I reminded her, perhaps with attitude, that she'd never shown me the ones Towns got. I'd seen them at Towns's office, though. She said softly, "Oh, yeah. Sorry. It's the end of a long day for me. Okay, I need to see yours. I could pick them up at your house. I'm leaving for home now if nothing else happens. Swing by?"

What could I say? I said yes, and thanks, and tried to remember if Chris would be home. Or Joe. I was creeped out enough that I would have been happy to have some company right now. Even my Dad. And just determined enough to protect them all that I hoped they would not be here when the sergeant arrived.

OK. Protect Chris. I would need protection myself from Joe's comments. Dad? Well, I'd been ignoring his since I was fourteen. I could deal.

Chapter Ten

I had barely enough time to manically pick up the living room, find the first letter in my desk, and check the whiteboard calendar in the kitchen. Chris would be home any minute. Joe had a client consult and would be home later.

I had an inspiration and quickly texted Chris. "Get takeout. Your choice. Charge $$. OK?" There was an instant "K," and I knew she would be delayed a little. Busy time of the evening for picking up takeout dinners.

Brew coffee? Pour wine? Snacks? That was my mother whispering in my ear. I told her ghost this was business, not social. No hostessing required. In reality, busy hostess tasks might have calmed my nerves.

Torres was there soon and found parking immediately in a no-parking area. I thought enviously that must be a perk of being a cop. We sat at the dining table, where there was good light, and I handed her my letters. She took some photocopied pages from a large envelope and compared them, handling my two notes very carefully.

"The letters Towns got. See? They do look similar. Not that I'm qualified to make that judgment, either, but just by eyeballing."

Yes, I saw. Elegant, old-fashioned penmanship. Copperplate?

Spencerian? Italic? I had no idea what it was called. It had never come up in my history studies. But it was similar.

"There's a surprise, though."

"Oh?"

She nodded. "New letters to Mr. Towns."

"Since I saw him? He told you about the one from the day I was there?"

She nodded again. "One more, even stranger. I brought you a copy."

Then she very carefully picked up my two notes and read them again. "Let me take these, show them to the analyst, get prints. We might need yours to compare." They went into a zippered plastic bag. She took a deep breath. "Honestly, I think this is to rattle you, and not more than that. Is it succeeding?"

I wanted to say, "Hell, no." Some dumb schoolyard bully notes? I really wanted to be that person, but I told the truth and admitted to being rattled.

"Well, it is bizarre. Here you are, acting like a normal citizen going about your business. You work in a museum. Not exactly a high-risk job. Homeowner. Taxpayer. PTA member? What could be more boring?"

I nodded. That's me, as ordinary as can be. Except for a few accidental adventures.

"Still. This is like a very vague, boogeyman type of threat. Know what I mean?"

I did.

"Interesting, maybe, that this is all so old-fashioned, isn't it? No email, Twitter, or anything else. Not even typing. Plain old paper. "

"Like it's someone old? Goes with the handwriting?"

She sighed. "Or maybe it means not a damn thing. Anyway, for now, please use more than usual caution. Keep your eyes open and wits sharp."

"I always do." At least I liked to think so. There were those who would disagree.

"And you must call me ASAP if you get more. Or if anything else happens, OK? I'm giving you my direct number. Keep it. Use it."

"I will.

She stood, collecting her possessions.

"Wait. I want to ask you about the fire."

"Do I look like a firefighter?" But she smiled when she said it. "Why do you think I know anything?"

"You said it. The police force is gossipy." I wasn't going to let her brush me off. "I'm betting you have sources in other departments, too? And it's your turf."

"Yeah, all true." She sat down again. "OK. I can say this. It's not our investigation unless someone is killed. So that didn't happen. But, yes, I know a few people. We overlap around situations sometimes, sure."

"And? Do they know what happened? Last public word was 'still under investigation.'"

She nodded. "True. They are careful and it takes time. Very picky work but, yes, they are treating it as arson. My friend says not a doubt about that. They are sifting through the evidence to lock in how."

"And who?"

"Working on it. Slow and steady. Arson cases are tough to solve. Why are you asking?"

"How could I not be interested? I saw it. I was right there. It was directed—okay, okay, maybe directed—at someone I care about. And landmarked property might have been destroyed. I care about that, too. I want to know!"

"You could have been a cop. You think like one. Give it a thought, if this history gig doesn't work out." She looked me up and down. "You might need a bit of boot camp physical training first." We both started laughing. "I'm heading off home now. Get in touch if you have any further thoughts on the letters? I'll be interested."

As soon as she was gone, I pulled out the new Towns letter, hoping to get somewhere before Chris came in.

The first ones I read in Towns's office had sounded like Louisa, much as I wanted to deny it. They accused him of stealing and of hypocrisy. I could hear her voice.

I started making notes, to refresh my memory.

Those letters appeared coherent in a way. Real sentences, real punctuation. It was only when you thought about the content, what those sentences said, that they actually seemed crazy.

Another reminder to myself: ask Torres if there had been some kind of psych evaluation.

This letter was different. It read like an escalation of craziness. Or a mind breaking down. More hateful words but even less sense. More random and even vaguer threats.

Maybe I needed to track down those biblical-sounding phrases, though. Maybe there was a theme. Then again, maybe it was complete nonsense.

Maybe I needed to put it all away for now. Chris was wrestling with the sticky front door and trailed clouds of delicious garlic and soy smells.

Later that evening I heard from Leary about our dinner with Louisa. He wanted me to pick him up in my car tomorrow night and chauffeur him over to the hotel where she was staying until her house was repaired.

That night Leary came out of his building on crutches instead of his wheelchair, looking determined. I could see it was hard for him, but he muttered something about standing up like a man. I also noted that he was wearing a jacket and a tie.

I was surprised he even owned a tie, let alone a jacket. He had shaved, too.

"You're all duded up tonight. Just how well did you know Louisa Gibbs back in the day?" I was teasing, expecting his usual grumpy response.

Instead there was a long silence and then a very faint, "Not as well as I would have liked. I was a kid then, young reporter. She was, oh, hell." He said it softly.

"Sounds like you liked her a lot. I am shocked."

"Shut up. She was like...like Katharine Hepburn in a movie. Know what I mean? A woman of the world. Certainly not my world. But I covered so many of her stories, we finally got acquainted."

I was pretty sure that was the most personal thing I'd ever heard him say.

Finally, I was able to choke out a soft "Would you like to tell me more?"

"No. Not at all." That didn't surprise me, but then he added, "I was real young, a raw kid from the outer part of the outer borough. You know?"

"I do. My home turf, too."

"To tell the truth, I'd never met anyone like her, then or since. Not afraid of anything. Didn't care what people thought. She looked like Mrs. Astor on the society page, but she could lead a demonstration like...like... I don't know. Lady Liberty on a poster, at the front of an army."

More interesting by the moment and shocking, too. Leary waxing poetic? I didn't think he had it in him. I waited, concentrated on the traffic, and waited.

"Not that she ever saw anything in me except a baby reporter kid she could feed information to. And she'd been married twice and wasn't looking for love anymore. She was more than okay with hero worship, though." My eyes were glued to the traffic, but I could hear the smile in his voice. "I was happy to have a drink with her occasionally and scoop up whatever she was tossing my way. She was using me, sure, though I was too green to know it, but I wouldn't have cared. It was like there was a special spotlight on her, all the time."

Leary in love? Or in awe? I couldn't tell, but it was a revelation either way.

"But you stayed friends?"

"Oh, yeah, more or less. On and off. After a few decades she saw me as a grown-up. I entertained her with stories about Brooklyn I couldn't put in the papers. She took me to fancy parties when she needed an escort, and I never turned down free booze."

"And you dressed up for that?" Impossible.

"She told me where to buy a cheap tux."

Leary owned a tux? Leary? Okay, now that really was the most surprising thing I'd heard.

When Louisa opened the door to her hotel room I saw her through Leary's eyes, hero-worshipping in a different way.

She shook our hands, but warmly, with two hands of her own. She was not from a hugging and kissing world, I guess.

She wore an old-style tweed suit and an even older style fur scarf, with the creatures' heads still on and little glass-bead eyes. My grandmother had one. Louisa was perfectly dressed for dinner out. In about 1956, I'd say. And she looked tired.

"How are you, Louisa? Holding up?"

"These last few days have been hard. Such a cruel thing to do to my poor old house." There were tears in her eyes, which she quickly blinked away. "And my life so disrupted. And the phone calls and more phone calls."

"A good meal will help. And may I say you look elegant in spite of it all?" Leary gently helped her into a worn Burberry raincoat, perilously maneuvering his crutches and waving away my help.

"What I need is a good martini or three!" She flashed us a rakish, unconvincing smile. I offered her my arm, and we crossed the street to a tiny neighborhood place with a gigantic menu.

The first martini was quickly supplied, and we had a few minutes of intense discussion about dinner. When Louisa chose a venison chop, I guessed maybe she really did need a good meal. Myself, I was overwhelmed by the unusual choices and relieved to find a burger. True, it was bison, served on a brioche bun, with house-made ketchup—you can make ketchup?—but still, it was a burger.

It was Leary who then said, "Now tell the truth, Ms. Gibbs. How are you managing?"

Her chin lifted. "I am managing very well, considering, and with the help of my wonderful Sierra. She packed up some clothes at my direction, and personal items, so I am ensconced at the hotel for the duration. I do have a good insurance agent, and the insurance company says they are expediting the settlement. Because of my age, they said!" She almost laughed. "I couldn't decide if I was insulted or appreciative! Nancy will start right away, and she says it is not as bad as it looks. More cleanup than reconstruction." She lifted her glass. "So there we are. It could be worse." We lifted our water glasses, too.

I seized the moment. "What actually happened that day? How did you get out without being hurt? I know Sierra was not there."

She suddenly looked grim. She put her glass down so hard some of the drink splashed out.

"Investigators have already asked me that. They say they want a full picture of what happened. They say."

Her hand was shaking as she picked up her glass and downed the last of the martini. "I have nothing more to say about it. To anyone."

Leary and I glanced at each other, puzzled by the sudden change of mood. He put his hand over hers.

"Louisa, what's wrong?"

She shook her head. "I don't want to discuss it. And I won't."

Our waiter came with plates, and she gave each of us a coy smile. "Let's enjoy these delightful appetizers, shall we? And do tell me, dear, how is your research coming along?" She was staring right at me, and I had to respond, but two could play at that game, keeping information close to the chest.

"I've learned a lot, but I haven't found anything that would help you. If I were to dig deeper into the building that was there before, get a footprint, find more plans on file? And ownership, too."

She tapped a fork on her plate in a nervous movement. "That

building was old, old, old. Probably built before there were plans filed and all that bureaucracy."

"Yes, that's true. But for later work on it, like updates, there may be records. You know I have to go with what I find, no matter how, um—unwelcome it may be?"

"Yes, yes. Do you think I am worried?"

I did, and I thought she should be.

"Since I know I am right, I am not. Not a bit." She turned to Leary. She was beaming like an uncannily determined yet flustered hostess, rotating conversational gambits to her guests. "My old friend, how are you? How is your health holding up currently?"

Old-fashioned dinner-party manners I had only read about.

"No, no, Louisa, that is one we do not discuss, remember?" He smiled as unconvincingly as she did. "And here is dinner. Would you share a taste of that venison with me? And which part of my duck appeals to you?"

She looked annoyed, started to say something, glanced at him, and stopped. She silently sawed off a chunk of red meat in red wine sauce and placed it on his plate. He responded with a duck leg for her, carefully trimmed, with a generous spoon of orange sauce. They each focused on their plates, but I caught them sneaking worried glances at each other.

As Louisa turned pink and tried to pour her third glass of wine, Leary moved the glass away and said firmly, "If you are in trouble, remember you are not alone. Do you have that clearly in your stubborn old head?"

Maybe it was her fourth glass, because she gave him a goofy smile, nodded, and announced, "Time for dessert. There is nothing like a slice of cake to banish problems."

Leary said dryly, "I wouldn't remember that, but you go ahead."

I didn't know what *mille-feuille* was, but Louisa insisted I try it, so we shared a large slice of crumbling pastry smothered in custard and raspberries. Not a bite was left. Espresso all around, a check grabbed by Leary—a first!—and I helped my elderly companions maneuver out of the perilously crowded room. Louisa insisted no one needed to accompany her to her hotel room.

"I am not a child," she said with exaggerated dignity. "I have my key right here." She did not, and we spent a few minutes helping her locate it in her coat pocket.

Leary watched until the elevator doors closed on her, and then he insisted at the desk that housekeeping check her room on some pretext. Any pretext would do. I saw some bills change hands, too.

He was entirely silent until we were halfway to his home. He was a guy who liked to talk. With authority. And some bluster. This was like chauffeuring a ghost.

"I don't know what she's up to." He never admitted uncertainty to me. "She wasn't just a firebrand. She could be extremely strategic. Polite word for *devious*. I'm trying to believe she's up to something now."

"Do you think it's something good or something bad?"

"Have I taught you nothing about the real world? You're still naive, cookie. I'm so disappointed." He wasn't. He was laughing at me. "Strategy isn't ever, itself, good or bad. All depends on what you think of the goals. Am I right? Which at the moment is difficult, as we have no clue about what her goals are."

I could hardly believe my ears. I glanced sideways, quickly so I could keep my eyes on the traffic. He sat slumped against my side door, head leaning on the window, a tired old man, not very well himself.

"I guess… I think…" A cab driver honked his horn—what nerve!—and I was distracted by his swerve into my lane. Even at night, Flatbush Avenue can be three lanes of aggression.

"Yes," I answered when I could. "She isn't entirely making sense, is she?"

We were at his building by then. I helped him out, and then it was my turn to watch from the sidewalk while he clumped painfully across the dingy lobby and got in his elevator.

Chapter Eleven

I went home that night preoccupied with Louisa. There was a possibility I had been trying not to consider. Was she—I called it "confused" in my own mind. Confused as old people sometimes become. I was not admitting, even to my own internal interrogator, to the more disturbing words. She was stunningly lucid at times, but at others, she seemed to fade at the edges. Was she just old and tired, or was there more to it?

By the time I was home, my brain hurt. My head hurt, too. I was happy to put all of this aside and be in my own life for the short time before bed. Chris irritated me, a welcome distraction. Dinner dishes were undone, and I was grateful. It gave me a reason to focus on doing something utterly mindless. Joe hugged me hello and went back to his own paperwork. Myself, I scrambled to lay out an outfit for the morning, and finally admitted to myself I needed more work-appropriate clothes. Would Chris like to walk me through some online shopping sites?

Normal life was pushing aside serious questions. There were no more letters for me that day. Maybe it was over. I was willing to believe that unless or until I had another letter.

I couldn't stop thinking about Louisa, though, and our evening out. She was all over the place, anxious yet determined to be social, defensive yet bossy. And Leary! He had obviously been shaken by the evening. I'd never seen him like that.

A few days later, she was back in her house. I finally gave in to my impulses and manufactured a work meeting in Brooklyn Heights, a complete cover-up for a visit to Louisa. I would see how she was doing and perhaps tell Leary. My excuse for dropping in would be to offer best wishes to her.

Before I reached her street, I had the flash that I should bring a gift, and turned back to the nearest grocery with a flower display on the sidewalk. A brilliant bunch of chrysanthemums later, I was trotting up the steep front steps.

Nancy answered the door, holding an old key ring in her other hand, toolbox at her feet. She didn't look happy to see me, and I'm sure I looked surprised to see her.

"Louisa didn't mention expecting a visitor. Sierra took her out to shop." She moved the toolbox to the top step. "I'm leaving. I was touching up the last bit of repairs."

I fumbled with the flowers. "I should have called. Somehow I just assumed."

"Oh, for crying out loud. Here! Give me those flowers, and then I'll lock up."

I lingered until she returned, hoping she could tell me how Louisa was doing, but her only response was, "Why don't you ask her yourself? I don't gossip."

She turned and walked away, but I followed. Of course I did. She was in better shape than I am, and walked faster. It's hard to be an astute interviewer when you're puffing to keep up, but I tried.

"Is Mr. Towns still bothering her?"

"Like I said...ask her yourself."

"I hoped you could help me understand. He seems to be a hardworking, worried, mild sort of old guy. But I also think he lied to me about the building they tore down."

She stared at me, but didn't stop moving briskly down the street.

"Could be. He is all of that. He is also hard-hearted and hard-headed, like all the leaders. Only one way is right and it's for sure his." Her expression grew harder with each word. Even her steps grew harder, slamming the sidewalk. She stopped suddenly. "Sorry, I have people waiting in here." She used a key to open the door to an old apartment building. She did it so quickly I thought she would slam the outer door in my face.

I never had a chance to ask the obvious. If she had left the Witnesses, and disliked them so much, why did she stay here, in Brooklyn Heights, where they would be so hard for her to avoid? That's not the way to leave a past behind. There's a whole big country out there. Just because some parts of Brooklyn are full of people who never left—that would include me—doesn't mean there is a magic boundary that no one can cross.

I stood there on the sidewalk, stumped about what to do next. I wanted to talk more. How could I make friends with Nancy? I had begun that sample chapter about Brooklyn Heights. Now that I had, my hard-won determination kicked in. It mattered to me to do it and do it well. And here she was, someone who connected a lot of different stories. She was involved in historical restoration. And at the most hands-on level. She did the actual work. She was a former Witness who had strong feelings about that. She had changed—really reinvented—her own life. And she'd lived in this changing neighborhood a long time. Apparently, she'd grown up here. I wondered what else she might know.

She was the perfect source for my chapter.

Maybe even the perfect subject, though I was pretty sure she would not want me to write about her. She could fill in a lot of background, though. I suddenly had the funny idea of introducing her to Leary. They'd either talk for hours or it would be hate at first word.

Amusing though that picture was, I reminded myself it was not what I was there to do. But what was that, exactly? Right now it was, unexpectedly, learning some more about Nancy Long.

When she had entered the shabby brick apartment building, I mentally filled in that it was for a job. Old apartments need renovation just as old houses do, and with so many of the buildings converting to co-ops, where the apartments are owned and at great cost, plenty of buyers are prepared to invest further in substantial work. Gleaming modern kitchens, stylish bathrooms with waterfall showers or soaking tubs—or both! Windows that look historically correct but are built to soundproof and insulate. All to transform that shabby apartment into a dream home. And for that, you'd want a first-class contractor.

All of this was so obvious I didn't even process it. I knew there would be work for Nancy here.

I stepped over to the lobby door to see how it looked and examined the panel of apartment bells. Chris went to school near here. Some museum staff lived around here. There was always a chance I would find a name I knew, a contact, someone who would tell me more about Nancy. Yes, I knew Louisa could, but I wasn't sure if she would. And anyway, I was right here, right now.

Not much of a lobby. More like a tiny foyer with an elevator beyond the inner door. No desk with doorman. Not "modernized" or "upgraded." Not even in good repair. The list of tenants told me nothing. About twenty names, Cohen, Baez, Armstrong/Park, Wang, Sun/Bello. A few were being used as offices. One name on the first floor had CSW after it, certified social worker. Probably a therapist's office. One said CPA/Tax Adviser. Another offered Nutrition Counseling. And one down near the bottom said N. Long—Assistance. That was not her contracting business name. This was—what exactly? I had no idea. Bad marketing? Or deliberately vague and evasive?

An appointment with a contracting client? Doubted it. Something else. If I could figure out how to use my phone to google things, I could look for this name. And with that thought, I vowed I would never, never admit to Chris I still did not know how to do that.

While I stood there punching buttons in frustration and trying to read that tiny screen in the bright sun, a skinny young man walked past me and into the building. I could see him push that bottom button, the one that said Long, and push the inner door when he was buzzed in. I barely made it in behind him before the door locked.

"Can you help me?" I said it to his retreating back.

He turned around. God, he was a kid, really, Chris's age or only a little older. Pressed jeans, starched shirt. He looked anxious, trying to be polite but afraid of what I could want with him. I was almost ashamed.

"I was wondering—do you live here?"

His puzzled look deepened and he turned pink, even his scalp. I could see it through the close-cropped, light hair.

"I was supposed to meet Nancy Long here, but I've forgotten which apartment or buzzer. Would you happen to know? "

"Uh, no. I mean yes, I know, but no, she has a meeting at her place now. Like, right now. I'm late." He was edging sideways toward the elevator. "Got to go."

Before I could say another word, he was punching the elevator button as if he was trying to hurt it. As if that would bring it faster. Before the doors opened, I managed to ask, "This is the address for Nancy Long, the psychologist?" He sure looked like a kid with a secret meeting. *Psychologist* could pass as a reasonable mistake.

"What? No, not at all. She's…" Exactly what I hoped would happen, but he stopped himself, turned his back on me, squared his shoulders. And then was rescued by the opening elevator door.

Well, hell. I had learned exactly nothing. I could not loiter here to see who else went in and out. I could ask a few questions, but first I had to figure out who might have answers. Louisa Gibbs was not answering her phone. Dr. Kingston was not available, either. I could try to pick up an online trace of something about her, but I'd wait until I was home and using a computer with a proper screen.

Now I needed to go home. And once there, I could also ask Joe what he knew. How would I frame that question? "Nancy Long? Is she involved with secret activities?" That sounded ridiculous even to me.

I left, walking toward the station, but turned back to make sure I had the right address. And I saw a girl, another teen, walking down the street at a swift pace, just below a run, her long braid swaying. Someone late for something. But she stopped abruptly at the door of the very building I was watching, looked around carefully and pulled off her long-sleeved T-shirt. Underneath she wore a skimpy tank top with a slogan. Did it really say, "Friends don't let friends join cults"? She stuffed the other shirt in her backpack and hurried into the building, still glancing around suspiciously.

This was most definitely a story, even though I didn't know exactly what story it was. After years of writing a dissertation, now I was supposed to write a story about life in Brooklyn. What it felt like. It would be worth figuring out what this story right in front of me felt like.

Thinking about it all the way home, I was no closer to an answer, and tomorrow would leave me not a minute to think any more.

But Joe was home early and the house smelled of chicken in the oven, some kind of one-pan meal with potatoes and carrots. I didn't understand it, but what bliss to find it there.

Chris was home, too, phone set aside, putting plates on the table. A glass of wine for Joe and me, a fancy gourmet soda for Chris. She said, giggling, "I like its aroma and full blackberry body."

"Have you been watching cooking shows?" My daughter? Impossible.

She giggled again. "No, but Jared's dad? He's a wine collector. Jared does it even funnier."

Joe had a story about his day, and then I threw out mine, the contractor with a mysterious secret. Telling it I thought it sounded like I really was telling a story, adding drama to something that probably had an ordinary boring explanation.

"I like that motto on the shirt. It's like, gutsy." Chris nodded emphatically. "Defiant. Girls who stand for something."

"Except for hiding it under her T-shirt?"

"OK. Yeah. So, um, maybe she wants to stand for something, but isn't quite ready to come out and say it?"

I found myself staring at my child, wise beyond her years. It was obvious now that she was saying it. I should have put it together myself.

"I don't know Nancy that well." Joe laughed at my appalled expression and went on, "She's known for great work, famous, really. That's all I've got, but I can ask around. Yes, I'll be discreet. Do you think I'm a complete yahoo? I have an architect pal who's worked with her company. But why do you care? Aside from the obvious?"

"That I am nosy?" I was smiling when I said it.

Chris said, "Yeah, that's totally it."

"What else?"

"I'll get back to you on that." She stood up, taking her plate to the sink. "But seriously, Mom. I thought Leary knows everything."

"Yeah. I don't know. Mostly, he does. But this is probably too current for him to know about. Besides, he looked pretty wiped out last time I saw him. I don't want to bother him."

Chris snorted and Joe shook his head. "You know it wouldn't bother him. It would cheer him right up."

"Go away." I flapped my hands at them. They were ganging up on me. "Both of you. I need to think. While I do dishes." I didn't really need to think. I needed to call Leary but, somehow, not admit they were right. It would take some strategy.

I did think it was too current. He was no longer reporting, and, sadly, many of his sources had died, moved to retirement homes, or left for warmer, low-tax states. Plus quite a few were not speaking to him anymore.

Later that night, Chris emerged from her cave and slapped some bright printouts on my desk. There were many pictures of T-shirts.

"You need new shirts? Not too expensive, I hope?"

"Always, but not from here." She looked horrified. "But look what I found for you."

A website I'd never seen. Leaving Faith for Freedom. What an odd name. It included a page for shopping. They offered mugs and pads and shirts, all printed with messages aimed at encouraging—who, exactly? There was no description, no "Who We Are" tab, but I was getting the idea. People who were leaving or were trying to leave or were disillusioned with a spiritual organization. Like Jehovah's Witnesses? Yeah, could be. They sold the tank top I had seen on the girl at Nancy's door.

Enough tiptoeing around. I found Nancy's business web page and called. I considered lying about a possible job, thinking it might get a quicker response, but I didn't. And I didn't tell her what I wanted to know, either. That might risk getting no response at all. In as firm a voice as I could summon, I simply said, "It's Erica Donato. I have some very urgent questions for you. Can I take you to dinner or breakfast? Please call me back, any time." I left all my numbers, home, work, cell, and my email addresses, too. "And I will follow up with a daytime call, just to make sure you got this. Thanks so much."

A gracious ending. A bribe of a meal. And a slight threat? Definitely. I hoped one of those might do the trick.

Chapter Twelve

It took a day of work, stopping to check for messages way too often, followed by an evening at home and an after-dinner walk to the supermarket, just because I was so distracted.

In the end, it was not my little bribe or my little threat that got a response. It was Louisa Gibbs, and I kicked myself for not doing that first.

Late that night, a call without even a hello. It began with an abrupt, "Louisa told me to talk to you. She says you are good people. I can meet for coffee tomorrow before work. I start work at 7:00." She named a small café on a Heights side street.

I said yes before thinking how much I did not want to begin a working day at 6:00. I'd have to take the bus or subway. I'd never find parking around there. Much as I dreaded it all, I was elated, too. Answers would be mine. I set my alarm, announced to my family that I would be out at the crack of dawn. I pretended I didn't hear Joe's "You? Up before me? Never."

It was so early the café was nearly empty. The caffeine-seeking crowds on the way to the day job weren't out yet, only the occasional early morning runner. Nancy sat in the back, her own large mug tight in hand. I ordered a muffin and an even larger mug, and joined her.

"What is it that you want from me?" Her words were wary, but her expression was not hostile. Or defensive. Then again, maybe I wasn't awake enough to read it. "Louisa said I'd be safe talking to you, but that depends."

"Would you like to share the muffin?" It was huge. I hoped she would say yes, but she shook her head.

"I have a long, demanding day, doing what I *am* comfortable with, in addition to this, that I am not comfortable with at all, so I had a great big breakfast before the sun was up. This is a favor to Louisa."

"I was so impressed to meet her. She was a big influence..." Instantly, Nancy looked impatient, and I stopped my babbling.

"I'm sort of trying to help her. You talked about the Witnesses next door. Can I ask you more questions?'

"That was my mistake. I never, ever talk about that. It's all in the long-ago past. I don't think...ah, hell, I'm here. Ask, but there's not much to tell. And no promises that I'll answer, either." She sighed. "The truth is that mostly they are good neighbors. I hate to admit that, but most people would say so. Clean sidewalks, fall and winter. Keep up the buildings well. How do you think I learned my skills?" She laughed at my surprise. "Not that they let girls do men's work, but I tagged around after my father, who was a master carpenter. Their way is to do every task the best way possible. And no loud parties and no garbage on the street, either. Like I said, good neighbors. And have you seen them with Louisa? Who is, let's face it, a little hard to disagree with?"

I nodded.

"Patient, right?"

I nodded again.

"Nicest people you would ever want to meet."

"But?"

"But they never, never, never give up, if they figure they are right. And they are never, never, never anything but right. Louisa looks tough, but compared to them, she is a noisy little terrier barking at a Saint Bernard." She took a long swig of coffee and helped herself to part of my muffin after all. "That's it. My take on what used to be my people. The end."

"Well, so. You think Louisa doesn't have much of a chance."

She looked amused. "Watchtower and a real estate deal? Did you hear what I said about never giving up?"

"How did you leave?" It popped out with no plan involved. I guess I really did want to know No, I was dying to know.

She leaned back with a hard stare for me. "That would take a lot more time than we have. And it was a long time ago, too. I'm not the person I was then. Hell, is anyone? Are you?" She looked straight at me. "Twenty, thirty years down the road from when you were a kid?"

"Not thirty years yet. But no, I'm not." I thought about it. "Not even close."

She shrugged. "What does the past matter now?"

"Well, I'm a historian." I tried a warm smile. "It always matters to me." I could make a whole speech about why.

She looked baffled. "What matters to me is what I see and hold and build. The details of what holds up a structure. Getting it right, the way it was meant to be at the start, well, that's a tribute to those old craftsmen. They left all the instructions there in the work, if you know how to read it. And yeah, yeah, some of that, the doing it right, is a Witness teaching. But my own history?" She shuddered. "Good grief."

I waited, looking as interested as I felt. The caffeine was kicking in nicely.

She shook her head again. "They're all about faith. Believing what you can't see or touch, because. Just because. You choose to."

"Because you want to."

"Yep. And I don't choose to. Or maybe it's that they're afraid to be in the world without that. It's too lonely."

"And you're not afraid?"

"Oh, hell, no, not of the things that worry them. I'm afraid of maybe falling off a roof. Or a boiler exploding. Reality." She was silent, munching more muffin. "Thanks for the muffin, but I have to get going. To look at replacing a boiler, as a matter of fact."

"One last question? Your business office is on Atlantic Avenue, so what are you doing in a building on Henry Street?"

Her almost friendly face shut down instantly. She shook her head and walked away.

So all I had really learned from my early morning effort was that Nancy Long had some secrets. Everyone I met lately seemed to have secrets. Even Louisa Gibbs, whose life only appeared to be all public. What a waste of a few hours of my sleep. And I still had a whole day ahead to keep my eyes open and my mind working.

I went through the motions very well. I wrote some memos, located important records for my architectural sculpture project, roughed out some copy for the exhibit about what these objects tell us about their time and place. Gave out intern assignments. Shared a joke with a colleague. It was sort of fun, and I knew I was doing it well, but there was a part of my mind processing in the background all day long, like a computer. I went over and over this newest of Brooklyn Heights questions. And how interesting a chapter I could write on my spec assignment if I could find some answers. And how I needed to do some more digging for Sergeant Torres.

No, I was not obsessing. Not at all.

Finally, I called Dr. Kingston. I could not confront Louisa. I could not bring myself to do it. But Dr. Kingston had studied Brooklyn Heights for years and years. He wrote the book. Literally. I had it on my office shelf. And he was a former professor, well known for liking to share wisdom and knowledge, as professors usually do. Sometimes to excess, as professors do. Anyway, he was more forthcoming than Nancy and more approachable than Louisa. At least I thought so.

He was there. He was not busy. He needed exercise. He suggested meeting me after work for a short stroll in Prospect Park near my home. Perfect.

We met at the park entrance, a massive display of civic sculpture in itself, located at the end of the even more massive circle of Grand Army Plaza, with its gigantic arch and multiple lanes of terrifying traffic. At the sight of his good-natured smile, stress from work, the need to accomplish things, deadlines, rolled away. He held two hot dogs from a street cart. Their unhealthy deliciousness, all garlic, crisp fatty skin, and mustard, would just hit the spot.

We munched as we walked into the park, shuffling the fall leaves underfoot. Runners passed us, a school team, and some bicyclists. The road was theirs, the park having long since been closed to auto traffic. It was ours too.

We turned to walk over a gracefully arched stone bridge. The sun was bright but low, and there was a bracing hint of chill in the air. I started to believe I might find a way through the muddle of my questions.

"So what's on your mind, young lady? Louisa hasn't been up to anything dangerous, has she? I haven't heard of anything lately."

"Not that I know about. They are sure she did not write the threatening letters, you know. But I have a feeling...well, I can't help thinking the cops are still keeping an eye on her."

"Without a doubt. Too bad, but she has brought this on herself by her feuding. It will all go nowhere. She's not a threat to anyone. She sounds fierce, but she's all bark." He looked at me sideways. "I assume you have already figured that out."

"I've been told that by others. Absolutely. But it's still reassuring to hear it from you too."

"And what else is on your own mind? Have you picked up anything about the fire investigation?"

"No, not a single thing. They say it takes a while, but I am so frustrated. Do you know anything? You seem pretty connected."

"Know? Not really, but I hear talk. No one believes for a second that it was an accident. No one. Last board meeting, no one could talk about anything else." His smile then was a wry one. "Not one item on the meeting agenda was addressed that night."

"Seriously? What do you do then?" I couldn't help being curious about how that could work.

"Send a memo telling them what was decided! They know I'm doing the deciding, but they're okay with that. But is there something else on your mind? Something about Brooklyn Heights history, hence your call to me?"

"Did you mind? I am so grateful to tap into your expertise." True, if also blatant flattery.

"It's yours for the asking. What's the question?"

"Do you know a renovation contractor named Nancy Long? "

"Everyone in Brooklyn Heights knows Nancy. She's very sought after. I've tried to get her to bring her expertise into the Historical Society but so far, no luck. She's not too sociable and says she hates meetings. Too much like her childhood. You know she was a Witness?" He stopped walking and gave me a kind of hard look. "Why do you ask? Surely she is not a suspect for arson?"

"No, no, certainly not. But I'd like to know more about her. She seems interesting. As a person? "

"Nancy? I *am* surprised. Usually she fades into the woodwork, and I've always believed it's her choice. The only interesting part of her is what she does with her hands. Her work is exquisite, I must say."

"So you don't think there is something more than what she lets people see?"

"Hard to say. You might have a point. But is what's there interesting enough to excavate past that surface?" He gave me another sharp look. "And you didn't get me over here merely for idle speculation, did you? What's really on your mind?"

"I think she's got a big secret."

"Nancy? Beyond her secret recipe for cleaning up stained antique wallpaper? I'm sure she's got one of those. And being raised as a Witness? And that's not even a secret, though she never discusses it. Believe me, Louisa's tried to pry out information and never got anywhere. She finally decided she'd rather have

Nancy's first-rate work than more ammunition for her fight with the Witnesses."

"It's something else." I thought about all she'd blurted out to me, and then regretted, and decided to stick to one thing. I told him about the building where she had disappeared, and who followed her into it. Did I have the address? Yes. I had a photo in my phone.

He stared at it for a while. "I know that building. I have a board member who lives there. I never ran into Nancy, though. She has her own very fine house on Orange Street and a warehouse and offices way down near the docks. It's not a one-woman operation by a long shot." As we approached a different park entrance, the one with the elegant panthers perched on stone pillars, he pulled out his own phone and scrolled to an address.

"It's my board member. I'll talk to her, and maybe she can tell you something useful. But may I ask why? What does it matter?"

"I don't know." His look then was so kind, yet curious, I had to backtrack. "I sort of know. It's this article I'm trying to write. A chapter, really." I was having trouble saying it. I felt pretentious, but then I gave myself a mental slap. Academics do write books.

Once I'd explained how interesting this story might be and what it could lead to, he smiled broadly.

"Good girl. Now is the time in your career to take every opportunity and run with it. We scholars—it's too easy to get lost in the research and forget about how to function in the world."

"But wait." I almost laughed. "Aren't academic politics supposed to be as vicious as anyplace else?"

"Or even more so. You know the joke? Because there is so little at stake! But jokes aside, you have a career now." He pointed to a bench. "Sit."

He took out his phone. "Hi, Gloria, it's Jeremy." Pause to listen. "Oh, fine, fine. I have a young lady here with a question about your building. Does Nancy Long have a place there?" A pause. "What? Hold. Hold! I'm going to put you on speaker." He fumbled. "Now say that again."

"She's a mysterious one." Her voice was humming with speculation. "She rents an office, and trust me, we all wonder about it. She's only there a couple of days a week, but then there are kids in and out. What the heck is that? You know, the building's a co-op. We'd all be responsible if there's a problem." Her voice went up. "*Is* there a problem?"

I was listening hard to the crackling voice as Kingston snapped, "What in the world are you talking about?" He made an annoyed gesture to me as he listened, a tap on his head. He thought the speaker was a little off center.

"Exactly what I said! Aren't you listening? Something is not right there." Her voice dropped. "What do you know? Anything?"

"Gloria, you are imagining things."

"I am not! People on her floor are asking questions." She gave a completely phony little laugh. "I'd suspect drugs, except for the fact that Nancy is Nancy. That's impossible, isn't it? But those kids seem so sneaky. You know, furtive."

I thought that all teens seem furtive. And yet, I wondered. I thought I might mention it to Torres. We said goodbye, and Dr. Kingston and I walked on to the street.

"I go this way, for my bus."

I thanked him as warmly as I could. I had liked him from our first meeting.

At home I collapsed in bed. A night of sleep, the comfort of a shoulder next to me, a cool room as the outdoor temperature was dropping toward late fall. That calm and energy from a long sleep lasted about five minutes in the morning. Before the day truly began, Leary called.

"You still looking at Brooklyn Heights?"

"Good morning to you, too. You woke me up."

"So? I have news. A body was found this morning in one of those Watchtower tunnels."

"What? Say that again! Are you sure?" He still had connections, still followed police news.

"You heard me. Early this morning. It might be on the news by now. But are you sitting down?"

"I am now."

"Dead man is a Witness bigwig by the name of Daniel Towns."

Chapter Thirteen

I couldn't help myself. Not that I tried very hard. I checked my calendar. No appointments today. I called in sick. Would I get into trouble? Did I care?

I didn't know what I had in mind. Those who say I'm too impulsive might have a point. Sometimes. Today? I felt attached to this street I had spent too much time studying. I could hear my stern dissertation adviser pointing out how wrong that was, that detachment was the only proper stance for a serious scholar.

"So what?" I answered back. Before I was a scholar, I was a Brooklyn girl. Detachment isn't our style.

As soon as I turned the corner onto Louisa's street, I could see the flock of NYPD cars two blocks away. An ambulance was slowly driving away, silent and dark. I guessed it was too late for screaming sirens and flashing lights.

The sidewalk was closed off by glaring yellow emergency tape blocking the entrance to the Witnesses dorm and the area all around it. People in uniform were picking up gear. This was cleanup. If there had been crowds earlier, bustling with excitement and curiosity, that was over now.

Not for me. I had been invited, right? That's what I told myself. I was, somehow, helping the NYPD. It was official. I knew "sort of" belonged in that sentence, but as I approached the scene, I refused to consider it. I was going with the idea that it was okay for me to be there.

But there were still a few cameramen around and a camera-ready local reporter. And Torres appeared. She didn't look happy.

She confirmed that Daniel Towns's body had been found in a Watchtower tunnel, but refused to speculate on how or why it was there. When the reporter stated the assumption that police presence meant the death was not natural, she nodded, but barely. She refused to speculate about cause of death, about a connection to the recent fire, or about any other question she was asked. She sounded terse, impatient, and stunningly uninformative. Now the reporter looked unhappy.

Torres was a master of the stonewall. I was impressed in spite of my frustration.

As I approached, a team in uniform was moving the tape to create a path for people to enter and leave the building. Torres was talking with a group of men in suits and gesturing firmly. Someone in a smart suit and stylish hair looked like he was trying to argue, and then Torres made it clear, with a chopping hand motion, that she was not accepting it. He didn't look like a Witness.

I wished I could get near enough to hear but guessed, when she pointed to the yellow tape, that it was related to access. When she looked up she made a small gesture, an acknowledgment she had seen me. As the men dispersed, she waved me over.

"As you see, I'm busy." She was scanning the scene in front of us even as she was talking to me. "Do you have any news for me?"

"I, uh, yes. Maybe." I handed her a folder. "I don't know if it is useful, though. It's all background."

She took it without looking and passed it to a nearby cop without looking. "Take it over to my bag." She hadn't turned to me. "That's it?"

She turned away to respond to the mic on her shoulder.

I had no place there. What a dope I was being to think I did. I should just leave, but before I did, I'd ring Louisa's doorbell. Just in case. In case someone was home finishing up the renovation. In case someone would talk to me. In case someone had news of Louisa.

Sierra opened the door a thin crack, saw that it was me, and let me in. "I am guarding against reporters." She had tears in her eyes. "They are already harassing Louisa." She put a finger to her lips and pointed. Louisa sat in the parlor with someone I recognized from the precinct. Torres's assistant?

She looked at me with a silent nod, and I went in.

I was disturbed to see Louisa looking extremely fragile. The detective looked determined and frustrated. Yeah, Louisa could have that effect on people.

"Hello, Detective…is it Kahn?" I sounded confident, but I was faking it. "We met when Louisa had her handwriting tested. How nice to see you again." I was aiming for convincing dishonesty. I thought Louisa needed a friend right now.

"Providing moral support again?" He didn't sound happy to see me. I didn't answer, just took a seat and put a friendly hand over Louisa's trembling one.

"I could ask you to leave." He sighed, a fed-up sound, and let it go.

"You're only asking me all these questions because I'm an easy target. Old and alone." Louisa squeezed my hand.

"Not nearly as alone as I would like. And, hell no, it's not because you are old. It's because you and the deceased were having a very public argument, a feud, and we need to know where you were last night."

"Why is that?"

She looked at him steadily, arms folded, mouth set, but I thought there was something else in her expression. Sierra, standing in the parlor door, where I could see her but Kahn could not, shook her head.

Kahn let out another exasperated sigh. "Look. There's been

a murder, OK? Not supposed to say that yet, but the gossip is all out anyway. And since you don't want to talk to me, I'm giving you the reason why you have to. Mr. Towns did not die naturally, OK? So we'll all be talking to everyone. You think we're targeting you? We're talking to all the people who knew him, the people who knew his routines, the people doing business with him, the people who found him, and the people who we know to have a beef with him. You know what that means, having a beef?"

"Young man!" Her eyes flashed. "You think that's a new expression? Don't make a fool of yourself!"

"Okay, okay. So you get it? So it's not an unreasonable question. We're doing our job like we're supposed to."

"Still, you are invading my privacy. None of your business, what a respectable senior citizen is doing of an evening." She took a deep breath. "I was home alone all evening."

"Can you prove it? Anyone see you? Any phone calls?"

"No." She stared at him until he looked away. "I was alone, like I am most evenings. I have nothing else to say." And the grim line of her mouth confirmed that she meant it.

"That's ridiculous. Ridiculous!" He stopped, took a deep breath, seemed to pull himself together. "I was trying to keep this nice. We'll come back with a team asking more questions. You want to make this hard? You have no idea what we can do." He walked out, then turned and pointed to me. "You. Come talk to me."

We stood in the foyer.

"Listen. You're a friend, right? If you can, talk some sense into her. She's got no reason to be such a pain in my ass, and my boss won't be too happy I didn't get answers. She'll be sorry, too. That is, unless she really is hiding something." He shook his head. "In that case, she's better off not making us mad by hiding it for long. Get what I'm saying?"

Yes, I got it. It was pretty obvious. The idea that Louisa was involved in a murder was absurd, but her behavior did look evasive, even to me.

He left with a slammed door and a reminder that he was not done. I seemed to have a job in front of me, to reason with Louisa, but when I went back in, she looked up at me with a strange expression.

"Don't even think it. They'll have to make me tell them."

"But..."

"Nothing to do with them, or Towns, or Watchtower. The truth was that Mr. Towns and I had been disagreeing for many years. True, I don't—didn't!—like him, but so what? What does it have to do with that body? Tell them that. And then I won't have to tell them about my own personal life."

I was pretty sure she was wrong about that.

"I'm very tired. Sierra, please help me lie down. No more company."

That was my dismissal, the only thing that was clear about this encounter. I left, completely baffled and at a loss as to what I should do now. Off to my real job? Call Leary and see if he had any insights? Not that personal insight was his strong suit, but he was smart and knew her well and obviously, surprisingly, cared. I tried, but there was no answer. Go find a fancy overpriced coffee and a doughnut? A really large one? That sounded more than tempting.

Life presented a different answer. As I went down Louisa's steep front steps, I could see Torres and Kahn in a conversation. Even from a distance, their body language shouted tension. She shook her head and opened a car door. I caught her just in time.

A pleasant smile. A tentative approach. "You two must have had a long day."

"You bet. Started this morning when it was still dark. And it hasn't stopped for a single second. We're winding up now, so we can have a break."

"I saw you from the steps..."

Kahn turned red.

"Tough young Kahn here had a little trouble with an old lady."

He turned redder when she added, "Lord, I get tired of training young detectives." She looked at him and relented a little. "When you take a dinner break, think of how else we can approach this." She stopped. "Not that I think she is the killer. But we need to know everything about that night, including whatever she is hiding. No excuses and no exceptions."

"So you don't believe her, either?"

"Oh, hell, no. I mean, it's not impossible, but it sounds wrong. Really wrong."

She closed her eyes, then opened them. "Hey, thanks for the material. I had more urgent things to handle today, though. Maybe tonight if I can keep my eyes open. Not freakin' likely, though."

"It's pretty random background. I don't know if you can use it. Maybe I could do better if I knew more about what happened?"

"Yeah?" I had a feeling she saw right through me. "What do you want to know?"

"Everything? I don't know anything except he was found in a tunnel."

"Yes."

"Where is he, I mean, his body? Where is it now? I saw an ambulance."

"Yes, that was him. Now he belongs to the ME. That's Medical Examiner to you. Autopsy required, absent any witnesses."

"He died alone?"

"Someone else was there." That was Kahn.

"Oh. The killer."

"That I can tell you, because, in spite of my best efforts, it's gonna be on the news tonight."

"So it's true that it was definitely not like a heart attack or something?"

The young man snorted but stopped instantly when his senior looked at him. He said, carefully, "Only in the sense that a bullet will cause heart failure. He also showed signs of physical attack. Marks on his neck, bruises, and so on."

"And it's also true about a tunnel? One of the tunnels connecting the Watchtower buildings?"

"Well, we don't mean the Holland Tunnel!" Great. A smart-aleck kid cop.

Torres gave him another exasperated look before she told me I had heard it right, that it was this building.

"Doesn't that suggest it might have been someone he knew, another Witness?"

She almost admitted that, then stopped and said, "We don't know yet. There are no damn clues, no one we've talked to so far saw or heard anything. They insist it would be impossible for one of their own to commit such a sin. And they are sure—sure!—it must have to do with the sale of their buildings. There has been resentment, they say, and even threats."

"Come on. That's impossible. A murder over real estate?"

I knew that was wrong even as I said it. Impossible? This is Brooklyn in the twenty-first century. Real estate can be a blood sport. Nothing is impossible,

"I don't get it. Aren't those tunnels heavily used? How could it possibly have happened there?"

"And yet, there he was." Torres sighed. "A few early cafeteria cooks were heading to their jobs when they found him first thing this morning. He was lying on the floor. He'd been there for a while. We could tell."

I tried to picture it but my mind wouldn't let me. A body in the clean bright busy place I had heard about?

"They covered him up with jackets, tried CPR, and ran for help. "

"And he was shot?"

"He was," Kahn confirmed. "Obviously not a street crime. No one had access to the tunnels except Witnesses until recently. And hardly any now."

"Now? What's happening now? "

"They say some contractors and so on have been down there.

With the buildings being sold, the tunnels will be filled in. People buying the new co-ops they're planning sure don't want secret tunnels under their buildings."

"So a few random people in and out. Can you track them?"

He grinned. "You bet."

"Like we said," Torres added, turning back to me, "there is a lot of conflict about those sales. So whatever you can pick up that gives objective background? Who knows? Maybe it will lead somewhere. Doubt it, but who knows? Kahn," she added, "go eat lunch and think up some new approach for Gibbs. We've got to do that better. I'm heading home for a little while."

I wanted to head home too, to sort out what I'd learned and what I'd given Sergeant Torres. There was nothing else I could do, I thought.

And then I ran into one more person I knew.

Chapter Fourteen

I ran into him literally. Or he ran into me. Working my way around the barriers, past the various personnel completing their work, he turned a corner, eyes on his phone, and slammed right into me. We had a hard, shoulder-to-shoulder collision, and I landed on the sidewalk.

"You're all right? Not hurt?" He helped me up. I hurt, but I could stand and move. "I'm meeting up with some people, but come along, I see EMS workers. I'll get you some first aid if needed."

He was on his way before I was fully upright. I limped along, struggling to keep up.

I knew him.

That was Mike Prinzig. I'd met him at his own home, with Joe, at that party full of real estate businessmen. The owner of the company buying up parcels of the Jehovah's Witnesses property.

My first thought was, "Would he recognize me in my dowdy work clothes?" That night I'd been dressed to shine. And a full dressing table of makeup! And my second thought was, "So what if he does not? What do I have to lose?"

I stood up straight and pasted a smile on my face.

"Mr. Prinzig?"

He looked at me with a question, and not a friendly one. Not the gleam of interest he'd had when I was more in party mode. This was more "Who the hell are you to be bothering me? I'll walk you to the EMS workers so you won't sue me, and then I erase you."

I put out my hand, smiled brightly, said, "I'm Erica Donato. Joe Greenberg introduced us at your housewarming party. This is quite a shocking day, isn't it?"

"Insane." He was already walking away, toward the building, with me trying to keep up alongside. "Do you have a connection here I need to know about?" He looked harassed, as everyone on this site did today. He didn't even pause in his stride.

"I am assisting Sergeant Torres with some background research. I am allowed to be here." I would stretch that story until it ripped. "Could I have a minute of your time?"

He ignored me as he turned to the group at the building door and announced, "Cops are done. I made them let us take a look."

I followed. He had said, "Come along," hadn't he?

Into the building, through the bland lobby and toward the back, an unmarked door. Two men and a woman in smart suits and a man in a decidedly not smart suit with an ID lanyard around his neck.

Crime scene tape was still up, but he told the cop on duty that Torres said he could be admitted. I stayed close and quiet. I was making myself as invisible as I could. The officer made a quick call and then carefully lifted the tape.

They were lost in conversation about due dates and payments, and seemed to have forgotten me. I wanted to make sure that continued. He opened the door, and I slipped in behind him and down the stairs.

I was in a brightly lit, shiny-paneled, linoleum-floored space that went on forever.

"It really is just like a hospital hallway." I didn't realize I had said it out loud until he turned around to me.

"What are you doing here?"

"You said to follow you, so I did." My story and I would stick to it.

"Did I?" He looked puzzled. "Maybe I did. This day has been too much, too damn much." His voice faded off but then snapped back. "Yes, it's like a hospital hallway. Were you thinking it would be like a subway tunnel?"

"No, no, I heard it was clean and bright." In my own mind, though, I had seen it as dark and mysterious.

"We're checking to see if it's back in order. One more freaking thing to be on top of until the sale is final, looking for anything that doesn't belong here." He paused. "And nothing belongs here. It should be a broom-clean passageway now." He turned and stalked off.

There were footprints everywhere. I imagined EMS and investigators of all kinds had been all over the place. And there was nothing else. An empty tunnel, just as it should be. And not at all what it had been a few hours earlier.

Picturing that, the dead man, his panic and confusion, I felt a little shaky inside. I'd lost someone that way. I didn't want to remember it here and now.

He came back slowly, looking satisfied. "A cleaning crew is coming in, and it will back in use tomorrow."

"What exactly happened here?" I tried to say it softly, not like the interrogator I was being. "Did anyone tell you?"

He was staring back at a spot down the hall he had examined. There were small blotches of brown along with the dusty footprints. Blood? I didn't ask. I waited.

Had he forgotten, again, that I was even there? Finally he said, "The morning teams, going to breakfast. He was right there on the floor. Sleeping, they thought, or passed out. He was already gone. Dead." He shuddered. "A terrible thing to happen here on our property. Almost our property. Only a few more papers in the way."

I blurted out, "A terrible thing entirely, isn't it? Dying like that."

He turned back to me, blinked, and stood up a little straighter. "I suppose so. But that's not my problem today. Must be the only one today that isn't mine."

"Come along!" He snapped it out. "We are done here. Soon this will be over and we are all back to our normal insanity."

"But." I had to say it. "But how did he die?" I said it to his briskly moving back, and he merely waved a dismissive hand over his head.

"Not our problem. Not our problem at all. Do we look like detectives?"

I was glad he couldn't see me behind him, because I was stunned at the ridiculous comparison. And the attitude.

"We now take back what is ours, return to our designated tasks, and proceed with our plans. Yes." With renewed energy, he repeated it. "Yes. Back to work. Too bad, but after all, he was in our way." He was talking to himself. I was sure of that. He nodded. "We couldn't get it done because he had to be nice. Fair!" I couldn't quite believe what I saw next. Thought I saw. He looked satisfied.

By then we were walking back through the building lobby.

I swallowed my disgust and politely stopped him. "Can I ask you one more question? It's not about this…this…incident. But you might know." I gestured around the massive lobby. "What was here before? Before this was built?"

"Nothing. Nothing worth remembering is what I heard from Towns himself. He was involved with this building. Before my time. They were run-down garbage buildings, due to be torn down by my old man or the Watchtower or someone else. So the Watchtower people only did a good thing with this piece of work."

He walked away without another word, off on his very important job. I stood on the sidelines and watched and wondered about Mr. Daniel Towns. His bland exterior hid some secrets. How many? A few? An attic full? His response to my question about what was there earlier was simply untrue. Or no, not untrue but not exactly honest. Not honest at all. Evasive? Was it possible Towns had forgotten a fire and the death of the three people? No. Not possible. Not at all. And almost as impossible that he did not know. He had told me he was here then. Had I misunderstood?

In the pleasant, sunny fall day, I had a chill. There was something here I did not understand. Actually, I did not understand anything that was here. The more I knew, the less sense it made, but I did know, somehow, that I had stepped into something much bigger than I expected.

Like any good historian, I heard that voice reminding me that the answer to that was ask more questions. I would go home and do that. Plow through what I already knew. Focus on what didn't make sense and plow some more. Track down someone who could tell me more about Mr. Towns's past. Surely someone—someone!—must know. Then tell Torres what I had found. If I found anything.

Was I still trying to put together materials for my silly ambition to write a book? I no longer knew what I was doing. I'd reached that point where there were too many questions and I wanted answers. That simple.

Not simple at all.

I had a job with a serious paycheck to take up my days. A teenager and a lover to take up the rest of my time. I'd have to squeeze it in, here and there, but I would have to. I was gripped by these questions in a way I could not explain or justify.

I worried about it all the way home, but I knew I wasn't going to let it alone. Or maybe it wasn't going to let me alone.

And so it didn't. It didn't let me alone while I watched a movie, as planned, with Joe. It didn't let me alone while Chris wolfed her dinner standing up and disappeared into a videoconference committee meeting. She explained it but I wasn't really listening.

And it didn't let me alone while I was at work the next day, doing actual work, getting absorbed, looking and sounding focused, but with my mind only partly there.

It felt much bigger than my job.

Finally I sent a note off to that Fitz. It was just a couple of paragraphs, sketching in a little background and listing out all the unanswered questions. He wrote back: "Damn! Real estate and politics and big money *and* a murder? Get cracking! I would read that in one evening, and I could sell the hell out of it. Do I have to make you do it? Let's meet IRL." IRL? In real life? "Forget this digital discussing. You work at the museum? When could you be free to meet? Any time works for me."

Part of me had been hoping he would say don't be ridiculous, you're not a detective, it's the worst idea ever. Write me something trendy about star architects. Something safe.

We agreed to meet outside my office, in the Sculpture Garden, tomorrow. He claimed to live nearby and work from home many days. That surprised me. I had him figured for a dignified older man, a refined Upper East Side type.

I made a list of all the people who would be open to answering questions. Or who might be. Or could be pressured to become helpful. Or could tell me some other people to meet. Even Prinzig the real estate man. I'd even dress up if I could get an appointment with him. I already had him pegged as someone susceptible to a polished woman.

If the detectives were talking to Watchtower dorm residents and Watchtower headquarters employees and not having much success, why would any of those people, devoted to Towns, talk to me?

And when I was done, I added Sierra. She might not know much about Towns. Probably knew nothing, but she might be a source of information for what the heck was going on with Louisa. I didn't know if she would talk to me, but she was young. She looked tough, but I'd learned a few things about being tougher from raising my own teen.

Chapter Fifteen

When I reached the chilly sculpture garden, there was no one waiting for me, only a skinny kid in a checked wool jacket, thumbing through his phone.

Then he stood up and called my name.

"Hi, I'm Fitz."

I took in his scruffy, stubbled face, carefully sculpted hair, and silly lumberjack clothes. What?

Yes, it was the right voice and accent. Preppy, I thought. Or Ivy League–y. But this kid? Younger than me? This is who had me so intimidated?

But he sure could talk. He plunged right in, telling me why I needed to move on this idea now with Brooklyn as hot as it was.

When he paused for breath, I looked at him. "How much do you actually know about Brooklyn? Have you spent any time here?"

"How can you even ask?" He looked proud. "I live in Bushwick. You can't get more Brooklyn than that."

It shocked me, how young he was. Bushwick became hip when more desirable neighborhoods grew too expensive for young people with a taste for adventure and no money. Up until then, it had been a run-down, charmless, dangerous neighborhood people tried to get way from.

Before I said anything else, he smiled less confidently. Even a little sheepishly.

"Okay, so I'm new to Brooklyn. Let's say the book would be for people like me, who don't know much but would like to know more. Whole armies of us. We can find the funky bars and great food, or even start our own, but honestly, some of us would like a little more insight. And so would the rest of the world. I mean you don't have to be dead to know Brooklyn anymore. It's completely the opposite now." He grinned. He was quoting a famous story.

OK. He was a kid, but he had read my mind. He added, "I didn't get to be an editor because the boss likes my hairstyle. I do know how to do this."

"Hmm. I get your point. And tell me why you think I can do this?"

So he did. He was pretty convincing. By the time he was done, even I was convinced. For the next day, busy with new ideas and a few fantasies, I overlooked one more important question. It caught up with me right in the middle of my working day.

Why was Louisa refusing to tell the cops where she was when Towns was killed? Was she just being ornery? Insulted that they even asked? That didn't seem too far-fetched, knowing her. I deeply wished I could take that idea, put it into a folder of answers, and label it Asked/Answered. Or better yet, Closed.

I could not, though, because the remaining question was whether or not she actually was hiding something. Involvement in Towns's death was too absurd to think about. I was sure of that. Wasn't I? But still. I looked at my list and circled Sierra' s name.

Finally, at lunchtime, I closed my office door and called Torres's number.

Kahn answered. He didn't sound happy to hear it was me.

"Yeah, sure I talked to your pal again. The boss came too, this time. We did our two-person act very smoothly."

"Is that like a good cop/bad cop?"

"You watch a lot of TV? Yeah, that's it, only smoother than they do it."

"And? And?" I might have smacked him if this was taking place in person.

"Not a word. She had nothing to say to us, and she said it. Nothing. Threats didn't work, and charm didn't work. But we know she's lying."

"Going on both your instincts?" I didn't know if he caught my sarcasm.

"Nope. Way better. We found a neighbor who saw her when he came home late from work. Saw her getting out of a cab."

"No!"

"Yeah. He's quite sure about it. So that sweet old lady is up to something. Right? And if you, or she, thinks we won't figure it out, think again."

He hung up on me.

Unbelievable, but then again, no, not entirely. I had seen her with Kahn, and something was off. Even I could see it. I was dead set on talking to Sierra now. How could I find her? No last name, no phone number, no address. I knew she did not live at Louisa's house. Hadn't Louisa said something about how Sierra made her lunch and left for her other job, leaving Louisa a cold supper? I took a deep breath and phoned Louisa's landline. And if Louisa herself answered, all bets were off. I would instantly hang up.

"Gibbs home. "

"Sierra? This is Erica Donato."

"Did you want Louisa? She is napping."

"Actually, I wanted to talk to you. Do you have a minute? I am worried about Louisa—lots of us are—and I wonder if we could talk sometime soon? Tonight, maybe? Dinner, my treat?"

"I don't know. I have to be at my other job, and I shouldn't talk about Louisa to people, and…"

"Louisa asked for my help." All right, maybe not exactly on this, but in general, she did. "And I like and respect her." Total truth, that. "It won't take long." Maybe true, maybe not. "Do you have time for a walk after work?" No time like the present. And I'd always found with Chris the secrets come out when we are doing something else. "Maybe a walking meal, like a food truck snack or an ice cream cone?"

"OK. I could do that. I finish here at 5:30? Meet somewhere?"

"I'll hustle right over. Clark Street subway station at 5:45."

There she was, on the sidewalk outside the station. She looked as nervous as I felt. We circled over to a doughnut shop and I hoped the sugar would help with the bonding.

"So you are Louisa's…what? Health aide? Housekeeper?"

"Whatever. She doesn't need health care. I take her to appointments, do some cooking, do some laundry. I help her with her mail and paperwork too. Part time."

"Oh?"

"Four days a week, afternoons." She started on a second doughnut as we walked.

"Important work, isn't it? How did you get into it?" I was breaking the ice. At least I hoped I was.

"I needed a job. I don't have family around here. I take care of myself, and trust me, there's always jobs in this line of work. "

"Like it?"

"Sometimes. I like Louisa a lot. She's a hoot. And she has no family to speak of, either. So we, like, provide for each other."

My opening.

"I bet she's not the easiest person to work for."

"Oh, hell, she's fine. It's great that she's right out there, all the time. And she's funny, you know? Snarky? And really smart. So she tells me all about Brooklyn in the old days, and I cook for her." She smiled fondly. "I've seen her ruin a frozen pizza. She can't cook at all. I mean, not at all. And I tell her about, like, living on my own, and tattoos. She can hardly imagine all that." She stretched out her bare arms to show off the maze of illustrations. Among the flowers and vines, I spotted a complex, three-part version of a Celtic knot and the heart-adorned words, "Loving Care for Loved Ones."

She saw me looking. "This matches one my friend Willow has. It's Wiccan." She whispered it. "She says it means woman power, so I wanted one."

"What about this?" I pointed to a leaping dolphin.

She giggled. "I just like dolphins. And see this?"

It was a magnificent sailing ship.

"For Louisa! Her family."

"I love it. I like her a lot myself. I'm worried about her now, though, and so are other friends. Aren't you?"

"Yeah. She's upset about the fight about her property, and she was upset about those mean old letters, and now she's upset about these cops and their dumb questions. Can't they leave her alone? They have no right to question her."

"Actually, they do. In fact, it is their job."

She gave me a look filled with scorn.

"I mean, like, really? Really? How could they think an old lady like that could attack a chunky guy like Daniel Towns?"

"You knew Daniel Towns?"

"Oh, yeah." She made a face. "Seen him talking to Louisa. Seriously, he was a pudgy old guy. In a fight with Louisa? Come on!"

"I like your style." She made me smile. "And I agree. But I've got to say it. She seems to be lying about that night. Do you have any idea what is going on? I can't help her—none of us can—if we don't know the truth."

"Nope. I wasn't there that night. Usually I don't work nights for her. I'm at my other job. And she didn't tell me anything about it. Not that she tells me everything, anyway. I mean, we're kind of friends but not like, sharing secrets too much. She has some, I'm sure. And I sure don't tell her mine. You know?"

I did know. She sounded like Chris. So we had reached a dead end for information, I thought. And we'd also reached her destination. We were in front of a large, bland brick building, sort of new, modern for the neighborhood, with a discreet sign: Downtown Care Home. I knew I had seen the name before, but didn't remember where until much later.

And the motto on the sign matched the one tattooed on Sierra's arm.

"Sierra, I'm so glad we had this talk." I was glad, truly, but I also thought it was time to use my mom powers, such as they were. I put a hand on her arm and gently but firmly made her look at me. I had a hard gaze looking back at her. "You need to tell someone if you learn anything, see anything, that doesn't seem right." My tone allowed no nonsense. "Tell me if you are afraid of the police."

"Not my place to tell anything." She stammered, then added with hostility, "Why do you need to know, anyway? You're not my mother. And I wouldn't tell her, either." The "so there" was implied.

"If it has to do with Louisa or with Mr. Towns, you'll tell me, or you'll tell a detective."

"If it would help her, I'd tell anyone!" Her eyes filled with tears, and I relinquished my mother of steel act. I wasn't very good at it anyway.

"Look. I'm sorry if I scared you." I handed her a tissue from my pocket. "There are too damn many secrets floating around. I can't figure out what goes with what. It's making me crazy. My whole job, my work, is piecing together the facts to see how they add up."

She sniffled and finally said, "But I would never do anything that hurts Louisa." The door to the building finally buzzed and she was gone.

I believed her about not hurting Louisa, but she was a kid in my eyes. How would she have the judgment to know if it hurt Louisa or not? Or, for that matter, helped solve Towns's murder or not?

As I stood there with my thoughts going round and round, and then around some more, a panel truck drove past. I dimly realized I'd seen it circling before, and then I registered the logo. Nancy Long's company.

A parked car moved away from the curb, and the truck slipped in instantly, not even struggling with the tight space. Nancy herself jumped out looking enormously harassed. Then she saw me.

"Ms.—I mean, Dr. Donato? I seem to see you everywhere lately." She was not happy about this. "I'm very late. I was trapped behind a dead car right in the middle of the Manhattan Bridge."

I was not moving. "We need to talk."

"No. Definitely no." But I did not move. "All right, all right, but not now. Can't now."

"When?"

"You won't give up. Am I right?"

I nodded my head.

"Later tonight, okay? Call me after nine?"

I didn't say a thing, but I stepped aside. Reluctantly

It was time to go home and try to drain off my frustration. I didn't realize until later that my emotions must have showed in my face. Joe and Chris were clearly avoiding me as I stamped around the kitchen eating their leftovers. That continued as I stamped on upstairs and closed my office door firmly. All right. Maybe I slammed it.

Nancy never called. Coward. She texted. "If you must, tomorrow at six-thirty a.m., same place. Only time I have."

I suspected she was trying to discourage me with that uncivilized hour. A challenge? Too bad for her. I set my alarm and went to bed.

She was there in the morning, corner table, looking bland and wide awake. I, on the other hand, probably looked cranky, tousled, and half asleep. I was in the right mood to take no prisoners.

"You had such an urgent need to talk?" Her voice dripped sarcasm. "I can't imagine why. I'm not that interesting."

"Oh, I think you can so imagine it." I loudly sucked down some more coffee, stalling until I was completely under my own control.

"I dunno. You like Louisa. I like Louisa. We both know Joe. I don't see anything to discuss there."

"I don't think it's about Louisa. I don't know. Everything seems to tangle up with her somehow, but no. This is about my efforts to write something about Brooklyn Heights. Efforts she supports, by the way."

I was happy to see she looked more unsettled now. Serve her right for setting up this absurd meeting.

"Well, what? And why me? I can't talk about any of my clients. Not if I want to stay in business."

"So you've built this business over time," I said, slowly and carefully. "You must have worked your ass off to do it."

She nodded, her expression the very definition of wary.

"I would guess, knowing a contractor well, that you maybe had years you didn't do anything but work. A woman in a usually man's field and on your own?"

Another nod.

"But that's not true now, is it? You're well established. Much in demand." I sprang my trap. At least I hoped that was it. "What do you do besides renovate old houses? In your spare time? You must have some now. What do you do in your other place, the one that is not your home or your business?"

Her voice said, "I don't know what you are talking about," but her eyes were full of panic. Secretly, I smiled.

She looked away from me, drummed her fingers on the table, and refused to meet my eyes. I waited.

Finally she said, "I was raised as a Jehovah's Witness."

"Yes. I remember. And you said something bitter about Daniel Towns."

"I shouldn't have. It was indiscreet. I'm sorry you remember it." Her voice sounded calm but her expression got harder. "I'd be lying if I said I cared about his death, and I know damn well I'm not the only one who has wounds he caused. If the detectives do their job, they'll get that, but me? I have a full life, in spite of him."

I was wondering what she meant, with my mind scattering in many dreadful directions. Should we even be having this discussion? Was I in over my head? How far over my head?

She looked up at me and almost smiled, in a mocking way. "Don't look so appalled. Not abuse but plenty abusive enough. His influence took my family away from me when I was still young. With them, you're either in or out. No questions, no gray areas. And he was already a leader, close to my very, very, very devoted family." Her calm voice was less calm with each word. "Disfellowshipped. That's what they call it. My loving family cut off all ties, and I was on my own unless I came back to their faith. So much for God's love." She stopped. Closed her eyes, opened them with no expression whatever. "So I built another life, one nail at a time, and the hell with them all."

I'd hit a nerve. A lot of nerves.

"I'm sorry. I didn't mean to …"

"Cut the crap. We both know you did. You wanted to ask questions. But nothing to be sorry about. Now you know. But it's my own life and not anything to do with his death or with Louisa, either. I eventually heard that old saying about living well is the best revenge. That was much later, 'cause that's for sure not how they think about things." The sarcasm was unmistakable. "But I did and I do, in my own way. Both living well and get revenge." She nodded. "Yes, I do for sure."

"What do you do?" I was fascinated, drawn in deeply by curiosity about how she had made another life. Perhaps because I had done it myself, when I became a widow at twenty-four. There is no story more compelling to me than one about reconstructing your life.

"I steal." She laughed at my shocked face. "No, no, no, not actually stealing. Get a clue! " She sighed. "You've been stalking me—yes, you have!—and I've spilled everything else to you. How did you get me to do that anyway? Might as well spill this. A little drop, anyway. I run a support group for kids who are thinking about leaving. Share my experiences and my, uh, learned wisdom. For what it's worth."

How had I not seen it?

"At the apartment building?"

She nodded.

She looked at me, the glimmer of goodwill gone again. "But you can't imagine I would tell you more? I don't tell anyone else's secrets."

"No, no, I know you don't. You protect their privacy, too, right?" I was also thinking this was perhaps a touch of paranoia.

"We're done here." She stood up. "I have work to do. I said more than I intended, and you got more than you had any right to expect."

And she was gone, just like that. I had work to do too. Did I have time to scrawl a few notes? One last gulp of coffee, a few lines in my notebook, and a fight with traffic to get to the museum.

Chapter Sixteen

I wanted to think more deeply about Nancy's extraordinary story, wishing I could get more details from her, in spite of her clear message that there would be none, and figure out how to fit it into my essay for Fitz. And I also couldn't stop thinking about Sierra.

My motherly instincts toward a youngster were battling with my curiosity and my concern about Louisa. I couldn't shake the belief she could tell me more even if she didn't know herself what it might be. Surely she must have stumbled on some of Louisa's secrets?

At the same time, I had badgered this young girl and probably frightened her. It's hard to see myself as scary. True, I can be mouthy, but I am a small person with a soft voice. Through Sierra's eyes, though? I would be an adult, brimming with self-confidence and authority. Maybe. Or maybe I was deluding myself.

Those were all the underground thoughts that rippled through my daytime responsibilities, no matter how much I tried to suppress them.

That night I asked Chris if I ever came off as scary. She gave me a strange look, started to laugh, then stopped. "You can be." She responded to my disbelief with, "Yes, you can. You come on sort of like, 'I'm here to take charge, and I'm taking names.'"

Joe came in then and added, not helpfully, "I think you are the scariest woman I know." He thought it was funny.

"What?"

"I mean it as a compliment." He hugged me. "My mom liked that song, 'I am woman, hear me roar.' Remember?"

"Oh, the Dark Ages. Geezer music." Chris making fun of both of us. "Actually, it's popular again these days. So, yes, Mom, you can be scary." She raised a single eyebrow. "But remember that doesn't apply to me. I know better."

Honestly, I was kind of flattered, but it did not help my dilemma. How to make Sierra talk to me without actually bullying her?

The answer that came to me was that I needed to check in again with Louisa, see how she was doing, and maybe ask her a few questions about her helper. A bonus would be if Sierra was there herself. It was a long shot, but it's not as if I didn't have plenty of reasons to talk to Louisa anyway.

The first evening with both Chris and Joe out around dinnertime, I made the call, and using my experiences with Leary, asked Louisa if she'd like me to bring over some dinner. She would. She liked everything, and dessert. She would welcome company, too. She would find me some interesting family artifacts to discuss. I deviously mentioned how useful it would be to have Sierra help with serving and cleanup.

Two days later, I arrived at her door, toting heavy shopping bags with baked pasta, meatballs, garlic bread, salad, a bottle of red wine, and a box of assorted cupcakes. Bribery at its most blatant. One of my areas of expertise.

And it paid off, because Sierra answered the door. She didn't look happy to see me, but I smiled warmly and lifted my bags.

"Dinner for Louisa. Did she tell you?"

"Yes. She said I don't need to leave her a meal when I leave for my other job." She did not smile or welcome me, only stepped aside to let me in.

Louisa called from the parlor. "Come right in. We have the

little table set up in here. Sierra will serve before she leaves. We are doing much better today. Sierra, how many days has it been since we heard from the police?"

"Two." She was reaching for the heavy bags.

I thought, they are not done with her, and wondered what they were up to in the meantime. Like investigating the murder from every other angle. Interviewing a few dozen other people. Forensics. Their job, in other words. Really, I knew that.

I greeted Louisa and followed Sierra downstairs to help unpack the bags. The kitchen was a warm room with French doors opening directly into the garden and a tiny old stove, enameled mint green, next to the modern one. I would have liked to explore—was that open space in the back once a large fireplace?—but that was not why I was here now.

As Sierra served salad on Louisa's dainty flowered china and poured the cheap wine into gold-banded stemware, I helped unwrap the rest of the meal.

"I did not mean to pry the other day." Yes, I did, but I'd intended more subtlety. "I hope I did not upset you." That much, at least, was true.

She was silent and unimpressed.

And then she started crying, the wine bottle shaking perilously in her hand. I took the bottle away, moved the wineglasses out of danger, and handed her a paper towel from the roll on the counter.

She sniffled and stopped. "My own family hates my life. They're all on a straight-and-narrow highway, and I was looking for some detours. Like the scenic route through the woods." She stretched out her tattooed arms. "I don't miss them at all. I don't." She sighed. "But I appreciate Louisa being like family. Anyone wants to hurt her goes through me."

"Wait! Are you one of Nancy's Witness runaways?"

Her look was almost comical. "What? Oh, hell, no. No. I was just dying in small-town USA. Ya know? I was looking for the bright lights. I got to know Nancy when she did a job at the home and I needed more work and she introduced me to Louisa." She jumped up. "Hey! Louisa's waiting for dinner, and trust me, she does not like to wait for her food. Here!"

She opened a door in the wall, loaded the plates onto shelves, locked the door, and pushed a button.

"Yeah! A dumbwaiter. Cool, isn't it? Those old-time dinner parties had acres of china and dozens of courses, so I guess this got it upstairs still hot." She leaned in to whisper a secret. "She showed me some of those old menus, and I didn't even know what the food was. Madeira sauce this and supreme that. Turtle soup? Eww."

Upstairs the plates were waiting for us, and Sierra set them up on the table in the bay window so we could eat and watch the activity on the street.

She was calmer and almost cheerful. I thought the tears had helped ease some burdens. That's a dynamic I knew from my own teen. She placed the cupcakes where we could see them, and reminded Louisa that there was a thermos of hot coffee on the sideboard.

When she was ready to leave, I walked her to the door to ask a question.

"You work at the Downtown Care Home?"

She nodded. "Night shift, mostly, after I leave here."

"I remember seeing flyers. I think. Was there a man who disappeared?"

She nodded. "It was so sad. Mostly he was my friend Willow's patient. He was troubled in his mind. Like, some kind of old breakdown maybe? Nice man when he wasn't having his visions." She whispered. "Willow thought he was an old Witness. Some of the things he said. But he wasn't too coherent."

"Did they ever find him? Was he all right?"

She shook her head. "They found his body. Near here, actually." She pointed to the benches across the street and whispered again, "Right out there. I didn't tell Louisa. He was sitting there, dead as could be. Not attacked or anything, just, like, gone. But I figured it might upset her. Got to run."

Shaken, I returned to the table to find Louisa had finished her meal and was anxiously eyeing the dessert.

"I couldn't overcome my mannerly upbringing. It would be rude to start dessert before you. But I was very tempted. Do come and finish eating!"

Scolded, I ate while Louisa watched the street and told me a few stories about grand dinners in the house, using this very china, when she was child. I wanted to record it all, but I couldn't quite bring myself to put a smartphone on the table with her elegant old silver and china. The garlic bread was incongruous enough, though Louisa didn't seem to mind. She ate three pieces right down to the crumbs.

I made a joke about the garlic, and she responded, "Don't be ridiculous. I'm sure it never appeared in my grandmother's kitchen, but delicious is delicious. Believe me, I don't want to live on lobster Newburg, and those cupcakes will be as tasty as Baked Alaska. Which Grandmama did serve for parties." She tapped her sterling silver fork. "I once had three generations' worth of silver service. Dozens of place settings and all the side pieces, too. Bet you've never seen grape scissors."

"You'd lose that bet! I worked on an exhibit about Gilded Age parties. But where in the world did you keep it all?"

"Up in the rooms that used to be for the maids who polished it! But I sold most of it many years ago to pay for a new furnace, and good riddance, too. When am I ever going to have a banquet for two dozen? I can't remember the last time it was used. A lifetime ago."

I gently confronted her about follow-up from the police. "Is it true, what Sierra said, that they are leaving you alone?"

"For now. They seem to be off invading some other person's privacy." She held up a hand to stop me questioning further. "And, as we are having a pleasant visit, we do not need to discuss any of this tonight."

I disagreed.

"You will have to answer their questions eventually. And Louisa? Why won't you? They will certainly come back."

"Don't think so. I have chased them away." She winked. I was unconvinced, but she put a finger to her lips and then passed me the dessert plate. The subject was closed for now.

I poured the coffee from the insulated carafe, and she invited me into the library, the room behind the parlor.

"I found something the other day that you might like. It turned up while I was looking for something else. If you promise to take very, very good care of it, you may take it home for a short time."

It was an album stuffed with both photos and keepsakes. I could barely get the excited words out, that I was a historian, worked in a museum, knew how to take care of such items better than she could even imagine.

"It was my grandmother's. I remember others, but I don't know where they are."

She'd bookmarked a few pages, including one showing a banquet table set with the very tableware we had just used. Twenty-four places at a long table, with three wineglasses at each setting and more cutlery pieces than I could count in the photo. There was a menu, too, elegantly handwritten, with seven courses.

As soon as I got home, I would attack this book. I could hardly wait. I would love looking, I do love looking, but more important, maybe some street views would be useful to my research. Or to Sergeant Torres.

"Louisa, did you ever look in here for early photos of your property? It might be useful evidence in your property dispute."

"Why, no. Does that sound foolish? I'd forgotten it even existed until I stumbled on it yesterday. Grandmama was not keeping legal papers in there, though. That was not her sphere."

"What was her sphere?"

"Do you need to ask? Fashion. Wait till you see the hats she wore. And giving parties."

We wrapped the book carefully in layers of plastic and put it in a tote bag. She chuckled. "Grandmama would be appalled to see her album wrapped in garbage bags. Not that she would ever know what garbage bags are. Or garbage, for that matter. She had a staff to take care of those messy details."

We had a final cup of coffee and admired the streetlights casting their glow.

"So many memories looking out at night. I did see the World Trade Center from right here, you know. And troopships out there when I was a young woman during the war." She pointed. "See that bench right over there? Someone died there. Not long ago."

That got my instant attention.

"Sierra thinks I don't know about it, but I do. I saw the ambulance and the police. Poor crazy old man." She looked at me and added, "Don't took so shocked. I used to talk to him sometimes."

I managed to croak out, "Tell me more."

"He'd sit there, all quiet and lonely, and disappear, and then come back. He was… He looked like he was homeless. Very shabby. We talked. Sometimes what he said didn't make any sense at all. Very, ah, apocalyptic would be the word. He would obsess about cleansing and sin. And then sometimes we just had a nice exchange about the weather."

"But wait. Why didn't you, or someone, report him? Get him some help?"

"He wasn't bothering anyone. Didn't beg. Didn't live there. Didn't do a thing but sit on a public bench like anyone else. That's what it's there for. And mostly if I offered any help he would turn it down. He took a bottle of water from me once, and an old straw hat one hot day."

"But I don't understand. He was the missing man from the home where Sierra works, wasn't he? There were advertisements about him."

"Oh, for heaven's sake. I didn't know that then. He never answered a single personal question. Never! He'd just babble nonsense if you asked. I didn't hear about those flyers until it was too late."

"But why didn't Sierra? She knew him."

"Guess she didn't see him." She made a dismissive gesture. "He was only there once in a while. Poor old guy."

She patted the album she had given me. "Now, my own ancestors mostly died right here, upstairs, in their big oak beds, and had grand funerals with big black cars." She stopped. "In the old days, there were carriages, and the horses had black plumes on their heads."

"Do you remember those?"

"What? How old do you think I am? Way before my time. But there were pictures. Some even in the newspapers. You know. Stories headed"—she made quote marks with her fingers—"'Passing of prominent local citizen.' I have them here somewhere. Now, my dear, it's time for me to go to bed and you to go home. Do you want to call a car?"

"No need. I'll take the subway."

"Keep that book under wraps then, until you are home safely, please."

Though I was itching to open it up as soon as I had a seat on a subway car, I had made a promise. But I didn't exactly keep it.

On the train, a woman smiled at me from across the aisle. I did my normal New Yorker five-second assessment. She didn't seem crazy, hostile, or begging. In fact, she looked respectable, older, quite a bit older than I am, friendly.

Finally, she leaned across. "Don't I know you? Did we meet at some historical society function? I used to work for Jeremy Kingston at the college."

My brain kicked in. "Oh, yes, now I remember. I'm sorry; it's late. We met at...was it the museum exhibit opening? When I worked at the Brooklyn History Museum?"

"Yes, that's it." She introduced herself and moved across to join me. "Nice to see you again. What are you up to these days? Still at the history museum?"

I told her what I was doing professionally and then, bursting with excitement, what I was carrying at that moment. I thought she would appreciate it, and she did.

I opened it to show her, grabbing miscellaneous papers as they drifted out from between the pages, and stuffing them back in. From a quick glance, it was a pile of a few catalogs, some letters without envelopes, a magazine. I stuck them back in to return to Louisa later.

I thought the woman would appreciate the photos, and we did a little shared squealing over a few. Her stop came too soon, and I bundled the book up to get ready to hop off at the next stop.

It was late when I got home, and everyone was in bed. I had a quiet hour to look at my loaned treasure. Later I'd make some notes, even catalog the contents if they turned out be useful. Or even better, important. For tonight, I would just browse. There are people who call *Vogue* or *Architectural Digest* eye candy, but to me, this was better candy than M&M's any day. And I do love M&M's.

I laughed. Louisa was so right about the hats. There were photos of garden parties and tea parties and departures on ocean liners, and everyone wore gigantic hats. Brims were as wide as the wearers' shoulders. They were covered with explosions of feathers or flowers or ribbons, or all three. A different style involved a crown so wide and puffed out I could not see how it stayed on a head at all.

How did anyone wear one of these on a crowded streetcar? I had a sudden flash of a comic moment like a silent film, a lady in a crowd with a wide hat causing havoc with a Charlie Chaplin look-alike.

And then I thought, silly me, these women did not travel on streetcars. Their private carriages had plenty of hat room. And on journeys, there were hatboxes at the top of the mountain of luggage. I saw them, right there in the photos.

Toward the end of the book, the carriages in the background became mixed with those quaint early automobiles. The clothing styles became a bit sleeker and more tailored, but Louisa's house looked much the same. It was built to last forever.

I put those loose papers back in the book for now, once again grabbing them when they fell at my feet. I wandered around the first floor ordering my home. And I went from thinking about the house in the photos, to the street in the photos, to the man on the bench across that street, facing that house.

I stopped and sat down, suddenly a little out of breath. Was that my story, the one I needed to write for Fitz? I was past the point of wondering if I should write one at all. He had convinced me. And here it was, the contrast between the beautiful facade of this house, this whole dreamy neighborhood, and real life as it is really lived. The elegant drawing rooms could conceal sad and ugly secrets. Edith Wharton told us that. And a man could die all alone on a lovely bench on a serene street. And a murder could happen next door.

Chapter Seventeen

When I woke up I could not shake the sense that I was on to something. It mystified me that it had taken so long.

After all, I am a historian. I know, really know, that the lovely clothes were cared for by underpaid maids sleeping in cells and waking at dawn to start up the fires. And were made by workers who lost their eyesight embroidering or were poisoned by dyes containing arsenic.

I know that the battles over building new houses and preserving old ones included snobbery and bigotry on both sides, and arrogance and greed to spare. Better angels were often nowhere to be seen during the infighting.

But somewhere in my mind, there was a thought—no, not quite a thought but a feeling—that the contrast that told the story most vividly for our time was the tragic story of a forgotten man dying in this pretty, privileged setting.

Or maybe it was my years in academia reminding me that even if visiting Louisa felt like a storybook, I damn well needed to watch out for romanticizing those misty photos.

Louisa's eyes were clear about the old days. My job was to be even more clear.

I planted my brain in reality. All my other questions were

hitting stone walls, but maybe this story unexpectedly taking shape was my story. It meant I needed to know more about the saddest part of it, the other man who died, the one who was not Daniel Towns.

Sure. Using my abundant free time after my real job, my child, and my lover. Chris was at the age where she preferred me to be uninvolved, so I needed to have appropriate parental watchfulness about that. Joe was my rock before he was my love, but I needed to remember things had changed. I needed and wanted to be all in but had to fight my tendency to become distracted and scattered. I'd lived life that way for so long, I guess it had become normal.

So. Breathe. Do my job. Be in my life.

But surely I could squeeze in a minute to call Sierra at work, couldn't I? To ask about contacting her friend at the nursing home? Couldn't I? Why wouldn't she want to talk to me?

Or maybe I knew enough to find her myself. Her name was Willow, not exactly common. And I had her workplace.

I keyed in the name of the care facility and added Willow. What I found was a long, annoying list of references to Willow Street and Willow Place, real locations in Brooklyn Heights. I added a string of words about "found dead" and "public bench" and browsing brought me a name. Jonathan Doe. Did that mean even the home did not know his real name?

And finally, a newspaper story about the dead man quoted a caregiver. Willow Lief.

No. Willow and Lief? Someone would actually give a child that name? And with it, a childhood of remorseless teasing? Yet there was a time, before my time, with a generation of children named River, Leaf, Summer and Autumn, Skye and Light and Rainbow and Saffron. Anything was possible.

Or had she chosen it herself, later? A new name for new life choices? I thought Sierra might have.

I would find out. Tomorrow. Tonight, dinner with my family. Paying attention where it needed to be paid. Chris updated me on the basketball team politics and produced information about a course to prep for SAT exams. I deferred on that, skeptical of extra costs. Isn't that her school's responsibility? I would confer with some other parents. She told me she would be in the park on Saturday, rain or shine, for a photography class assignment. I didn't remember being so busy at her age. Or, to be honest, so ambitious.

Joe and I caught up over an after-dinner glass of wine after Chris disappeared into her room. It was nice. Cozy, even. We stretched out on the sofa, legs entwined, Joe working on his laptop, me reading the newspaper. He agreed that the name Willow Lief was highly suspicious. We went upstairs early.

I tackled Willow Lief in the morning. I had it all planned. Introduce myself. Mention the book I was theoretically writing. Interview her about Jonathan Doe? If I believe I have a purpose, I could make other people believe it too. That was my plan.

I didn't anticipate the assistant on the phone who said, "Oh, she isn't..." then stopped and coolly said staff members are not allowed to tie up the office line with personal calls.

I politely asked for a supervisor, and she said they did not give any information about employees, of any kind, ever.

When I tried to justify my questions, she snapped, "You must understand, we protect both our employees and our patients."

"About that," I said, and mentioned Jonathan Doe.

"Oh. No. No, I certainly cannot talk about that. We are not allowed to discuss that with the press at all. Our attorney..." And then her frosty voice faded off uncertainly.

"But I'm not the press so maybe you could ..."

"No."

And then the phone went dead after the loud sound of someone slamming down an old-fashioned handset. Was I once again being scary? She was unhelpful and even worse, unreasonable.

It makes me angry to hear no for no good reason. All right, I am not stupid. I could guess that the facility might be in some trouble for losing a patient as they evidently did. A lot of trouble. Her attitude was not personal, but I didn't actually care. I had a story to write and send to Fitz, and this was a piece I needed. Even if I wouldn't know exactly why until I had the whole story.

Could Sergeant Torres put me in touch with someone who had investigated that death? Probably. It might even be her. Would she talk about it? I had no idea. Probably not, I admitted grumpily. Why would she?

I had work to do this morning, but I was on a roll. One more effort and then to work. I texted Sierra. "Need to talk to Willow Lief. Please help." And then, before I hit "Send," I added, "Counting on you." I had turned to guilt, a mother's necessary tool. And then I started my actual work for the day.

I carried my phone with me to lunch, just in case. I wrote out a page of questions for her, if I ever found her. When I found her, I told myself. When.

Finally, there she was. "Axed her to call U. On leave from job." I threw myself into one more hour of work and then hit the keyboards again, searching for anything I might have missed about the death of Jonathan Doe. That turned out to be exactly nothing.

This was not going well at all. Then my phone buzzed just as I was getting ready to leave. Text message coming in. "Willow here. Sierra said call. Don't like to talk. What?"

Text? Could I clumsily text the subtleties to someone already hostile? I stabbed in "please call." And she did.

By then I was too psyched and simultaneously too unnerved to calmly tell my story about who I was, a harmless scholar, and the story I was trying to write. I rushed through it all, babbling, I was sure.

She was completely silent. I barely heard her breathing. The only thing that made an impression was when I said, and repeated, that I was not an investigator or a reporter, that I only wanted to know a little more about Jonathan Doe.

"Not allowed to talk about patients." She muttered it. I could barely hear her.

Then she whispered, "But I'm gonna lose my job anyway, so ha-ha, why not? Screw their rules. Yeah."

I said, very carefully, "Would you like to talk right now?"

"No, got to get out now. Where are you?"

I told her and assured her I could get anywhere I needed to be.

"You know the health food store on Seventh Avenue? I need to get some herbal tonics. Very stressed. Very, very. Meet me in half hour?"

Yes, I could do that, easily. She was gone before I could ask how I'd know her.

I was on the alert for someone Sierra's age and style who would be on the alert for me. I was startled when a voice from across the aisle whispered my name. I hadn't noticed her before, a woman much older than Sierra, much older than me. Actually, she was plain old. She was short and chunky, with oddly assorted drab layers of clothing, many chains around her neck and wrist, and long gray braids. Decidedly eccentric but not that unusual a look for the health food store.

Her shrewd eyes looked me up and down as she whispered my name again and added, "Willow here. In the flesh."

I made a belated attempt to pretend she had not startled me.

"Thank you for meeting me. Is there someplace you'd like to go to talk?"

"I haven't eaten today. Treat me to a veggie burger, and I'll overlook the smell of cooked flesh. Any nearby place will do."

I made an "after you" gesture and followed her down the street to one of our many local fancy burger restaurants. It was late afternoon, early evening, actually. And she hadn't eaten. Was she sick? Had she slept all day? Was she abusing something? Several somethings? She had that look, of something being way off.

She ordered her burger topped with soy cheese, and then

demanded of the young waiter, "What do you have in a natural drink? Herbal without added sugar."

He stood up straighter and reeled off a list, assuring us they were all sourced from organic producers. Willow questioned him further and made a selection of ashwagandha. I had no idea what that was and was relieved to learn they also offered soda, fully caffeinated and sugared.

She looked me over in silence for a long time. "I can tell you need something calming, not that sugary junk. Linden tea would be a help, and valerian, especially if you have trouble sleeping."

This from a woman who had a tremor in one hand and eyes rimmed with red. She did not look well at all.

Did she read my mind? Because she said, "I have self-prescribed the ashwagandha for myself. Exactly what I need to get me right."

She did not say another word until our food arrived. She tore into her burger, and I wondered how long ago her last meal was. At last she sat back, looking a bit more alive.

"You bought me a meal. I owe you more than a tea prescription. What do you want?"

"I'd like to know about that a missing man. Jonathan Doe? Sierra tells me you cared for him, before he got lost."

She turned a little pale and gulped down the last of her tea.

"I didn't know you would ask me that. I wouldn't have come. His tormented soul is resting in peace now. At least I ask the universe for that every day. I still have that much faith."

I was feeling a little like Alice here, lost in a backward world. Could I anchor her to what I would call reality?

"Tormented? Is that why he wandered off?"

"That's a ridiculous question. He went on walkabout for whatever reasons buzzed in his head. He had some days when he was almost in his right mind and others when he was living on another plane of existence entirely."

Oh, boy. What did that even mean?

She saw my face, I guess, because she added, more kindly, "In the medical words used at the home, he had episodes of being delusional and schizophrenic. It never mattered to me what the words were. We care for them and love them either way, try to keep them fed and clean and as well as they can be." She closed her eyes, as if it all became too much for her. "Bastards. They blame me. Not failure of their security, oh, no. It was all me. I was with another patient. If I hadn't been, believe me, I would have talked him right down. No one there does it like I do. But you know, they gotta have a scapegoat. Old, old ritual that is, scapegoating."

She looked as if she was slipping off into neverland herself. "He could be a sly old guy at times. Very clever, some of them, in their dementia, very calculating. He found a way to slip out of the building. They asked and asked me how he did it." She smiled slyly. "I didn't tell them a thing, because I don't know myself."

I wondered what she did know.

As if hearing the question I hadn't asked, she said "I knew him as well as anyone could, considering that he didn't know who he was, and some days didn't even know who he was pretending to be. But there were times. Well, I sat with him at night and he'd be awake and we'd sit and talk. If he wasn't up to that, I'd read him back to sleep, but some nights he'd be talking away. Some nonsense, and then something that almost made sense. Almost. He talked a lot about the old days."

"Did he? What old days? Tell me more, please!"

"Yeah, well, you couldn't always tell if old meant last week or last century. In fact, most of the time he didn't know himself." She leaned toward me and whispered, "But I thought he had something on his mind, those last weeks before he disappeared. He was, like, more agitated. More happy, sometimes, and then more upset. Docs said it was his dementia progressing, but what do they know? It's us, who see them day to day, that *know*. Something was worrying him."

"What was it?"

"Who the hell knows? Couldn't make head or tail of it. But there was something. I know it in my heart."

"Who was he? Did you know that?"

"Nope. Never did find out. What they told us is that some Good Samaritans in his building found him passed out—that's all I knew about how he came to us—and those neighbors, they didn't know much more. He kept his self to his self, is what I heard. I mean, I don't know if the front office got more on him after a while. And when he wasn't raving, he didn't have a lot to say that was real personal. In fact, nothing."

She leaned back and stared at me. "I think that's a veggie burger's worth of talk. I'm dry and I can't drink alcohol anymore, so I'm heading home for an herbal tea with some energizing essences." She gave me a wobbly grin. "You ought to try it sometime."

"But wait!" I blurted out it out before she walked away. "I wanted to ask more about you, too. I'm trying to learn all about Brooklyn Heights."

She snorted. "You mean like Loweezy Gibbs, the great? Yeah, yeah, little Sierra tells me stories. And besides, I knew her when. But, yeah, I have been hanging around here a few decades. More than a few. But memories are not my thing. What's gone is gone."

And with that, she was hustling out, bumping into tables as she went. I'd lost her for now, and I was kicking myself, but deep down, I knew I'd find her again. I was getting good at this.

It wasn't until a few days later that she texted to say: "You want more? I have papers. His bench at seven p.m."

Chapter Eighteen

Was I being jerked around? Why, yes. Yes, I was. I didn't like it, and I hadn't liked this Willow person so much in general. Was I going to be on that bench before seven o'clock? Nothing would keep me from it.

She was there, waiting, her arms wrapped around a plastic grocery bag. The sky was dark already, and she looked as if she was nodding off. I spoke her name, softly and then sharply, and when she didn't respond, I felt a little tremor of fear.

She opened her eyes.

"Knew you'd show up. I can read your aura, you know." She looked up at the nearby streetlamp. "We got enough light here, I'd say. I didn't want to do this someplace all bright and public. It's strictly between us." She patted the bench. "Sit, sit."

"You have something to show me?"

"I do. That there." She pointed to the bag. It was bursting, with rips in the plastic, and sticky with oily stains. "Gonna give them to you. They are not safe where I am, and like I said, you have an aura. Jonathan Doe. Poor old guy. You ever see him?"

"I might have. Right here on this bench."

"Skinny as a needle, he was. Lost some teeth, too." She smiled. "He used to go in and out."

"You mean mentally?"

"No! Well, that, too, sure. But no, I mean he went in and out of the home. He found a way. Not supposed to, but he did. He liked a little walk around outside. He'd forgotten a lot—like his name!—but he always knew how to get back home." She shook her head. "Always a giant cosmic puzzle, what they lose and what they hold onto."

I had no idea where this was going. I figured saying "Get to the point" would not be helpful, so I tried to hold her wavering attention.

"But didn't he end up really lost? "

"Sadly, yes." Her voice shook a little. "He ran out of…I don't know, whatever it was that kept him anchored that tiny bit. But see, I knew him. I know he was happy being out on the street, however rough he was living. Free. A free man. But then I think, maybe I should have told on him before, and he would've lived longer. Then, maybe, he wouldn't call that living, anyway." She sighed deeply, sadly, looking out into the darkness. "Hard to tell what he would have thought, since he wasn't exactly thinking anymore in the usual sense of the word. Mostly he was off in some parallel universe. That's what I believed."

She leaned in toward me. "He wrote crazy stuff. Real interesting and mystical, even, but crazy by our reckoning, anyway. He scrawled and scrawled on those papers. Illustrated them, too, with pretty good sketches. Sometimes he'd give them to me, like, for safekeeping. Like they had any value. I saved them. And no, I don't know why! I never knew myself. Seemed like maybe they had meaning, and the reason would manifest itself."

She was starting to sound as crazy as Jonathan Doe. I was wondering how soon I could get away.

"Long, long ago, some young kids, students, came to the home and recorded people's stories. You ever heard of doing that?"

I wanted to laugh. I'd listened to many tapes like that and seen transcripts, too. Oral history has become a terrific tool in my world.

"So he was so off base, even then, that they didn't keep what he said. She was kind, this kid, and listened like she was learning something, but then she tossed it away after. So I kept it, too. Figured, I dunno, it might come in handy for something, sometime." She chuckled. "Like maybe there'd be a miracle and he'd get his mind back and explain it all."

"Wait. Are you telling me you have his tape here? And those sketches he did?"

"No, no, no." She smiled. It was not a warm smile. "Where did you get that idea? I said papers. These scraps I collected. Very weird, but there are secrets hidden in there. See what you can find. If you do well, maybe—maybe!—I'll find that tape for you."

"What are you talking about?" It came out louder than I intended. "Is this a game?"

"Game?" She was unruffled. Her voice was soft. "Game? Hardly. But I need to know if you are the right person to hold the secrets." She looked down, spread her fingers, and examined her nails with an air of complete indifference. It didn't fool me for a second.

"I'm too old for this." I stood, keeping a tight hold on the shopping bag. I thought she might try to take it back. "And you should be too. Cat and mouse? Not me." And I walked away, stomping down the block. If she wanted something, let her chase me.

Possibly I ruined the dramatic effect by sneaking a look back before I turned the corner. She still sat there, looking steadily in my direction, in the dim streetlamp light. She saw me. I know, because she lifted her hand in a gesture of, well, something unknown. Hail? Farewell? Dismissal? Respect?

Oh, who cared, I grumbled to myself as I went on my way. I had no patience for this nonsense. And I still had the papers in the plastic grocery bag, for what it was worth.

I was not hopeful, and that turned out to be a good thing. When I looked them over later that night, it was like going through someone's overflowing wastebasket. There were sketches, amateurish, with monsters, people with scary faces, dark smoky landscapes. Pages torn from publications. Written pages that were random scrawls, phrases, nothing that told a coherent memory or story or even a chronology.

Even at first glance, I felt in the presence of a damaged mind, as expected from a man who was so lost. But what was going on in Willow's mind that she saved them? Could I suppress my desire to shake her, hard, to force her to spill what she knew? I'd have to, if I wanted to talk to her again. I didn't think my mom skills would work on her the way they had on Sierra.

My brain must have worked on while the rest of me slept, because I woke up with a new idea. One faint thread in those scrawls was familiar. They talked about fire.

I carried the bag to work and locked the office door. There was no way to organize that bag of papers the usual ways, by date or subject. Not even by physical format, as the papers were a mess of legal pads, torn-off off scraps of other pages, printer paper, school notebook pages, colored construction paper. Some ink looked faded, some pencil writing was badly rubbed. They had been written over a long time.

Completely random kinds of paper in random sizes. All I could do was make a pile as tidy as possible and get to work.

I made working copies and highlighted and set aside every page that mentioned fire. I tabbed the ones that had something of additional interest.

And when I was done dealing with a stack of almost trash, there it was. Something. I didn't know what exactly, but the phrases about fire were the same as some of the writing in the letters Towns had received. Not mine. Not Louisa's. Only his.

My hands were shaking as I looked for Sergeant Torres's number and pushed the buttons. My voice didn't sound like me when I left her a message. She cut in live before I was done. When I had told her, there was a long silence. She was a cautious woman.

"That is certainly interesting. And strange. Don't do anything, okay? Don't discuss with anyone. Don't do anything with the papers. You're at the museum? I'll be over soon. Less than a half hour."

That's how I found myself with Sergeant Torres in the museum café, hoping no one I knew would see us there, using a larger table to spread out the pages.

She looked at all the pages I had set aside. She took out a folder and pulled some pages from it, laid them next to what I had given her, looked some more. She did not say a word. I fidgeted, looked at my phone, waited, wondered if a cup of coffee would calm the butterflies in my stomach.

Finally she covered her eyes and shook her head.

"Sweet Jesus! This is something for sure. And I can't ignore it. A week ago I would have said I don't even have a case to work on where this fits. We were only looking into the letters Towns got, and the Mrs. Gibbs ones."

"And mine."

"Yes and yours, but less heavyweight. But none of it, even added together, hit the level of crime. Now. Now, maybe it relates to his murder. Or not. It's real cluster of a mess."

"Wait! Are you sorry I brought them to you?"

She gave me a look that was mostly exasperation. "Don't be ridiculous! I asked for your help. Remember? And whatever we have, we need. We've got something here. And one other thing?"

She turned two pages around for me to see. One was Jonathan Doe's scrawling, one a copy of one the letters to Towns. Side by side, even I could see it right away. She looked smug when I gasped.

"They're the same handwriting, aren't they?"

"Looks like it to me. We'll have to get our expert over to confirm. But."

I was having trouble getting the words out. "Could this be it? Could he be? I mean, is this?"

She sounded amused. "You're stuttering. And yeah, that would be nice and neat except for one little thing. I don't remember for sure, and I have someone checking, but I think this derelict guy died before Towns."

My next words were a curse. Her response was "You got that right. But it's not nothing. We'll see where it goes." She started tidying the papers and putting them into her folder, marked set first, then the rest.

"Wait a minute! I can't give you those!"

"You're kidding, right?"

"No." Her impassive appearance made me nervous. "No. They are not mine to give away on some whim."

"They're possible evidence in a murder investigation. I can do whatever I think I need to do."

And here I thought we were friends. I should have thought this through.

She softened a tiny bit. "I get it. I know. Unintended consequences. But it was the right thing to call me. And your contact will have to live with it. By the way, I need to know more about her, too. Everything you know, in fact."

"Nothing." I was embarrassed. "I don't know anything. I have a cell phone number. And she used to work at Downtown Care Home. She is on leave, and she did say she expected to be fired. And that's it. I don't even know where she lives or, maybe, her real name."

She gave me a sharp look.

"Willow Lief? Hard to be believe that's for real, don't you think?"

She nodded. "The rest, leave it to me. We'll track her through her job."

"They wouldn't say a thing. In fact, they sounded kind of panicky."

"Oh, they'll talk to me."

I had a moment of wondering what it would be like to walk in with a badge instead of a polite request.

"You got names of who you talked to? And Ms. Willow's phone number. Unless the phone's a burner, we might get to her that way too."

"I have a request. A favor," I said as I wrote the information.

"Yes. Probably."

"What?"

"You want to know what we learn, right? Once this is all over, I'll tell you all I can. No promises, though."

She left. I still didn't like it that she had taken the originals, though I knew she needed to if they were to be analyzed. But she didn't know I had made copies of all the ones I thought were important. It's always good to back it up, right?

And I had Ms. Willow Lief's phone number. How could I make nice to her after our last encounter? My fully justified, unwise little tantrum? I could tell her to expect a visit from NYPD's finest. She would be so grateful for the heads-up that she'd spill everything I wanted to know.

Or she might vanish. She was that ornery. And this was now part of a serious investigation. How much trouble would I be in if I meddled? Even unintentionally? No, Erica. Bad idea.

Or I could offer her food. She'd all but licked the plate at our first meeting. I silently thanked my long-gone mother, whose instinct was to smooth any interaction with food. She was not above using it as a bribe, too.

I called; I left a message, a pleasant invitation. I completely ignored our little kerfuffle. Never happened.

And then I waited. I finally gave up work as a lost cause for the day. I was so antsy I could barely sit at my desk, let alone concentrate on a museum project. Instead I laid out my copies of Daniel Towns's threatening letters and Jonathan Doe's crazy notes. I copied out each similar phrase.

They weren't merely similar. They were the same. They must have had great meaning to Jon Doe—they came up again and again. Obsessively? Did they to Towns, the recipient of the letters?

A page from an old book, saved and highlighted in glaring green, said: "the scriptures refer to Jehovah as a consuming fire... He annihilates those who set themselves in opposition to him." And on another "the devil and all those not written into the book of life will be cast into the lake of fire." That page spoke of the symbolic meaning of the phrase but that was not the part he kept highlighting.

And he wrote and illustrated, "sorcerer's portion will be the lake that burns with fire," "He came to baptize you with fire," and "Lord your God is a consuming fire." "Astrologers and stargazers are like stubble the fire will consume." That one was illustrated with a chart of some constellations on fire. And "he that is taken with the accused thing shall be burnt with fire." That one was written in two colors and vividly illustrated. It looked like someone's nightmare.

And there were articles on the dangers of witchcraft, heavily highlighted. He circled the phrase, "peril of coming completely under the control of the demons."

He wrote of other things, too—the pile even included photos of kittens—but as I slowly dug through the mess, witchcraft and fire as punishment kept coming back. It was an obsession that held him tight. At least that is how it looked to me.

No one at Watchtower would talk to me, I thought, if they wouldn't even willingly talk to the police who were trying to solve Towns's murder

It was a long shot, but I was glued to my office and I had a computer. I wondered what my friend Google might have to tell me.

As it turned out, a lot. The Jehovah's Witnesses' major task was to communicate their beliefs to the rest of the world. That's what the giant publishing business was for, and they were tech savvy too. Look for Witness beliefs online and there was be plenty to read. Lots and lots and lots. And I am skilled at looking.

Some tentative experiments with "fire" and "witchcraft" and I found all Jonathan Doe's words, with the biblical citations for many of them. A lot from Revelations but some from the Gospels, some from the Old Testament, and some from Watchtower publications.

Time to ask Leary to tell me another story about the old days in Brooklyn.

I didn't call. I scooped up the papers, left a note on my office door that read "Family emergency—call my cell if necessary," and walked out the door without a pang of conscience. It was a while before I thought about what that meant. At the time, my only thought was, "Leary never goes anywhere. I'm going straight there to pound on his door."

When he heard my voice and opened the door, I said, "Tell me a story. It should have witches in it."

He pulled back in surprise, then laughed at me and said, "Are you sure you are spelling it right?"

"Always the smart aleck!"

"One of my better qualities. So seriously, why witches? And is that what I owe the honor of this surprise visit? I would've baked a cake if I knew." He was still teasing me. He doesn't know how to bake a potato, let alone a cake. And he can't eat cake.

"Look! Look at this." I threw the papers on his table and spread them out in the right piles. "Take a look and tell me what you see."

He sat and looked. I sat and fidgeted. Then I got up and fidgeted. I was so anxious to see if he saw what I saw. Then he said, without so much as looking up from the papers, "Sit down and quit fidgeting."

Finally—finally!—he muttered, "This is some strange stuff. Been a long time since I read anything that, um, weird? Delusional? Where'd you get it?"

I explained, just enough to make him understand.

"Witches, huh?"

"Don't you see a connection?"

"Go in the office, look around the second set of cabinets, third drawer up. Under Brooklyn Heights, you ought to find a subfile."

His apartment was a pigsty, but the room where he kept his work-related files was precisely organized and immaculate. He didn't even need to look to find any topic, anytime. I often thought it said more about him than he would have wanted to put in words.

There was the file. "Wise Women Kraft." I knew it would be there. Inside there were a few handwritten notes, a couple of typed pages, and a few clipped articles. A blurry photo.

Back in the living room, Leary was leaning back in his wheelchair, eyes closed.

"You asleep?"

"Not at all. Thinking back." He snapped up. "What do you need? My papers or my memories?"

"Both." I folded my hands. "I'm ready for my story, please."

"Now who's the smart aleck? Well, I knew them back then. Handful of women in a sort of commune. Worshipped a mother goddess. Or THE mother goddess, they would have said." He smiled. "In some circles that was kind of trendy around then. Ya know? Rejecting the patriarchal old religions and getting back to the original deity, the Great Goddess."

"What?"

"You're surprised? It was kind of feminist and kind of that woo-woo, mystical thing. Tarot, astrology, crystals, alternative health, meditation. The whole nine yards."

"Was it for real? Any of it?"

"You mean, real as in 'real'? Or you mean real as in true believers in a thing you can't prove? And what religion does not fit there? I should know, being a recovering Catholic myself." He smirked. "Spent my whole life recovering."

"Both, I guess."

"Both is right. Lots of hocus-pocus flimflam, like astrology. Come on! But some believers too. They read a lot of mythology, some guy named—hell, I can see the book cover. Bachofen! And they liked these ancient little statues of chubby women from ancient digs. Those files there? Those woman there at the store did believe in what they were doing. Friendly, welcoming bunch, on the whole. Free meals one night a week. Strictly vegetarian and organic, so lots of lentils, but they meant well. Homegrown honey. Herbal medicines to sample. Lots of pamphlets on healing. Talk your ear off on the Way, the Great Mother, the moon, the lines of power." He shook his head.

"But Leary? I mean, I don't get it. Were they convincing? Did you get it?" I couldn't imagine it.

"No, I did not. Not them and not the Hare Krishnas and not the pope, either. Skeptic head to toe, that's me. But if you went in? Ah, it was nice. They always had smiles, soft voices, time to explain anything. Oh, yeah, and they took karate, too."

"What?"

"Part of their creed. Peace didn't mean being a victim. Brooklyn was a rough place then. People tried to rob them a couple of times. They put one in the hospital." He smiled. "Very tough, but sweet in every other way, too. All other ways. Rejecting patriarchy and its rules, ya know? Women owned themselves. They should do what gives them pleasure." His smile got bigger. "Who was I to argue?"

"Are you saying what I think?"

"Yep. I wasn't always old and crippled. Normal young guy, nice looking too. Ex-choirboy making up for lost time." He winked. "They had parties. With vision-creating substances. And doing whatever felt good, whatever made you happy." He smiled. "It was the times. So we got happy. A lot."

I thought about it. The women. A new kind of woman? And what else was going on then. How it looked to Leary. And how it must have looked to someone from another worldview. Warm and welcoming? Life affirming? Or the creation of Satan?

And how do you deal with that? Cleansing. By fire.

"What happened to them?" I knew the answer. I wanted to hear it in Leary's words.

Chapter Nineteen

"It burned to the ground. Gone, poof, in a couple of hours. How'd you miss finding that?"

"Don't be insulting. You know I didn't miss it. But I want to hear it from someone who remembers it."

"OK. Yeah, burned to the ground in the night. It was falling-down old, held together with tape and chewing gum, more or less. In the store you couldn't exactly tell that, what with all the posters and incense and—I don't know—scarves over the walls. Hangings. You didn't notice the cockroaches in the walls and the ancient plumbing. So it went up in flames one cold night. They thought it was the ancient coal furnace. Or maybe candles fell over. They were always lighting candles in there."

Something in his face? His voice?

"What are you not telling me?"

"I had my sources. Yeah. Friend from the old neighborhood was a fireman. It wasn't what they said in public, but they knew it was set. They knew it, but it was hushed up until they had some leads. And then they never got any."

"You mean, it really was never solved? I couldn't find anything."

"Yes, Cookie, that's what I'm saying. They never got anywhere on it."

"Did they even try?"

He shook his head. "I wasn't connected enough then to find out." He stared at me, shrewdly. "Think hard. You wanna bet a few people did not like that decrepit old pile in their pretty midst? And a few other people did not like that shop for a few different reasons?"

"I get it. Bad influence on kids? Offense to religion? Immoral?"

"All of the above. And wild, liberated women, all lawless and disrespectful and loose. And all hairy and dirty and sexy on their pretty little street, too?" He snickered. "Bare feet on city sidewalks? Not exactly Saks Fifth Avenue style, right? Start with who hated them. How many places do you end up?"

"So they died? The news report said an old woman tenant who didn't hear the alarm and the two women from the group—the co-op?"

He grinned. "They would have said coven. And man, it's been almost a lifetime since I said that word or even thought it. But yeah. Them."

"So you knew them well. Was there anyone special to you?"

"You mean like a couple? They didn't believe in pairing up. We all hung out. It was all go with the flow of the moment." He seemed to be looking far into the distance. "Good times. Harmless, no matter what people thought. White witchcraft. Ya know?"

I didn't, not really, but I would find out someday, maybe. But today I had other questions on my mind.

"Do you remember names?"

"Come on! After all this time? And it didn't matter, 'cause they all had their special names. True names, they called them. Kinda like playing dress up, which they also did. Flowery flowy outfits and, I dunno, scarves? Turbans? Those names were all misty and mythical, too, like, ah, Nimue or Galatea or Morgana."

I tried not to smile.

"And nature names. They loved those. I remember one cute kid named Starry Sky."

"Not really!" I tried not to laugh.

"Damn straight really. And Autumn. And Echo, maybe?"

And Willow? Then I knew. I knew. Why had it taken me so long?

I would find Willow Lief and shake her misty, aging self until she told me everything. If I could find her.

I would find her.

As I stood to leave, Leary said, "One more thing. I'd forgotten this."

That stopped me short. "*You* forgot something?"

"Hey! I've covered a few thousand other stories since those days. And yes, maybe my memory of those days was fuzzed up by a certain amount of partying, too. You don't know about that. You were always a grown-up. This. There was a letter nailed to the wreckage after the fire. Something like 'spiritists defile the people and should burn like stubble.' Like that."

"Wow." I sat down again with a loud thump.

"Yeah. But they never got further on that, either, far as I ever knew."

Oh, yes. I would find her, if I had to camp on the steps of Downtown Care until they coughed up an address.

In the end it didn't come to that. I saw her on the street, a block from the health food store. I followed her in, keeping a discreet distance, and watched her as she slid from one of the store's shabby connected rooms to the next. After a furtive glance around, she slipped a bunch of fresh herbs into her shabby tote bag. Then a bottle of medication. An item from frozen food, and after a fast look, a second one.

While she was absorbed in shoving her items to the bottom of her bag, I silently slipped up behind her and snaked a hand out to grab her arm. She gasped, but I held tight.

She turned and glared, hissing, "Let me go, you…you scorpion. I'll scream for help."

"And will you tell anyone about the items in that bag, buried under your jacket?" I did not loosen my grip.

She went limp, wilted, almost collapsing, and I still did not let go. Beaten, she stood upright and whispered fiercely, "What in the name of the Great Mother do you want from me?"

"The truth. The whole truth this time. Am I getting it or do we have a talk with a manager? Or I can walk you over to the cashier and pay for your items?"

She closed her eyes, as if praying and whispered, "You win."

We stepped into the last aisle and checked out, with some awkwardness, as I would not let go of her while I pulled my wallet out and threw some crumpled bills on the counter.

On the sidewalk, she gasped, hyperventilating, or faking it very well, and begged to sit down. There were benches across the street in front of the school.

"If you cut and run," I said as firmly as I could, "I will run you down. I'm young enough to outrun you. Count on it."

We sat until she recovered herself. She did not try to run. She could barely speak. Finally she said, "You got me. Now what?"

"Now you tell me the rest about Jonathan Doe and the Wise Women shop, everything you left out before."

She actually flinched. "How'd you figure it out?"

"That doesn't matter." I didn't owe her that. Or anything. "Cough it up, and I'll buy you dinner."

She almost smiled. A bitter smile, but still.

"So you said. OK. OK. That shop, that group..."

"Coven?"

"Oh, be serious. You don't know enough to use our words. Yes, it was my home. Then. My family. Yes, I was one of them. We only did good. The natural power of the earth and the Great Mother. We taught love."

"White witches?"

"Some people use that term We didn't. But yes."

She stopped. I waited.

"We were free women of power. And some people, some evil scared ones, couldn't accept that, the freedom or the power. So yes, we did have our enemies. We ignored them except for sending loving, uh, meditations, their way."

"Spells?"

She looked annoyed. "I said meditations."

"Were they men?"

Her look was pitying. "What do you think? But women too. If you spent your whole life worshipping the rule of the sky god father, how do you think we'd look?"

I knew. They looked like the negation of everything such women lived for, believed, thought, valued. Demeaning of their truth.

"Like witches. Like danger. Whose fate is fire?"

She nodded. "We never knew. Never found out." Suddenly her eyes overflowed. "They were my family, my tribe, my home. We lost two sisters that night, and the family scattered, looking for safer places of stronger power."

"Back to Jonathan Doe, please." Actually I wanted to know more about her whole life—who wouldn't?—but I didn't know how long I'd be able to hold her misty attention. Back to business.

"Jonathan remembered us. So strange." Her face went from weepy to dreamy. "Every so often he was back here in this world. And then we talked about the old days. He remembered us, in bits and pieces. The bowls with shiny crystals and smooth stones of power, the agates and turquoises. Our lovely herbal scents and the leaves that helped with visions. And the girls with soft skin and dark eye makeup." She teared up again. "My sisters."

I was beginning to feel trapped by nostalgia in a world where I didn't want to be. I imagined—I think it was imagination—a whiff of incense.

"There's more, isn't there? Stop wasting my time!" A thought struck. "Do you know who he was?"

"Even he didn't know who he was, but he dropped hints about who he used to be. Our sisterhood, we were the forbidden fruit to him. Big time. Ya know? He remembered, one time, how scared he was when he first came by. He came to give us their newspaper and save our souls." She gave a harsh bark of something like laughter. "Can you imagine that scene?" I could now.

"But he learned we were not as he feared." She shook her head. "We wouldn't harm any living creature. We caught mice in safe cages, and carried spiders outside on a scrap of paper. But you know? The pagan idea disturbed some poor lost folks."

Enough.

"I want that tape you told me about. No games."

She smiled at me. Not an entirely nice smile.

"I have it right here. Whatever I care about, I keep with me. What's it worth to you?"

Oh, really? What was it worth to her? Me not beating her up right here? Me dragging her over to Torres's office for—I hoped—a brutal interrogation? She had a real talent for releasing the worst in me. I wondered if her sisters were like her. Yet another reason for people to hate them.

Who was I turning into? So I did the opposite.

"You know you want to give it to me. You meant to all along." I can be sly, too. "That's why you told me. So enough fun and games."

She nodded. "Smarter than I perceived. Let's see if you're smart enough to work out the secret." She dug into her bag and handed me videotape. At least I thought that's what it was. An antique. And while I was examining it, she disappeared. She was there and then she was not. Not on the street in either direction. Nowhere on that block for her to hide. She had vanished in plain sight.

No, not magic, white or any other kind. That's all bologna. Complete flimflam in my hardheaded opinion. But I did wonder how she did it.

I stared at the tape, knowing I had nothing that would play it. There were places that could convert it to a disc or a computer file. Sure there were. An old-time camera shop nearby had been staying in business, barely, by doing that kind of thing, but I was impatient. The college-age son of a neighbor had a room full of audio equipment and DJ ambitions.

I rang the bell. He was home. I explained, sort of. He didn't need the whole story. He said, "Nothing to it. Come back in a few hours." Then he asked about Chris, was astonished that she was already looking at college, and that was that.

I did a few errands, had lunch, and cleaned up my office a bit. And in less than a few hours, I had a playable DVD.

A raggedy-looking man, not so old but battered, sat at a primitive camera setup and answered questions from an unseen interrogator. Video and sound quality were terrible. It was early days for do-it-yourself video technology, and oral history projects were usually done on a shoestring anyway. More like a frayed shoestring.

He gave his name, but it was garbled. Damn! I wondered if a fancier conversion could pick it up. I had no idea, and no idea who would pay for it, but I made a note.

They asked him questions, starting with a few simple ones to establish who he was and where he fit into the project. And nothing made sense. I was so disappointed, as they must have been, too.

For his name, this time he rattled off three. Good Lord. But I did stop the disc to jot them down. He admitted to living in Brooklyn Heights. Sometimes. Asked for an address, he mumbled for a while. The only clear words were "here and there." And then he said, "Once it was Bethel."

Bethel was the Witnesses' name for their community in the Heights. So. Now I knew something but it was almost the last thing I learned. He mumbled. He rambled. He sang. And he ranted, too.

I could see why the interviewer didn't want it. It was useless for her purposes.

It wasn't until the second watching that I picked up how often he mentioned fire. And it was the third time that I was able to catch some of the Bible passages. Between the crackling, poor quality recording and his incoherence, it was torture to get the verse numbers.

It was the fourth time that I finally caught a name. Not his name, dammit. And deciphered the mumbles. He looked straight ahead and said, "Why didn't you help? Before I tried to baptize them and refine their souls by fire. And saw them burn because they were women who profaned themselves. Before I did all that. I was so scared. I wasn't well. Brother Daniel, I was lost in my soul. You were supposed to be my guide, my friend."

And he started to cry.

Chapter Twenty

I was shaking. I needed to talk but there was no one at home. I could not reach Sergeant Torres, but I left her an urgent message. "You hired me to find some background information? I think I just did."

I could not reach Leary. Where could he be?

But there was one other person who must remember some of this. Maybe all of this. I had not asked her because she was not—how could she be?—an objective source, but there was no one else. I couldn't sit at home chasing my thoughts around and around my brain.

I called Louisa. She answered herself, was glad to hear from me, invited me right over. And with the help of a car service, I was there in twenty minutes, door-to-door. Damn the expense. Torres could pay for it.

I found her sedately having a cocktail with Dr. Kingston. There was a plate of dainty puffy things to go with it.

"Come right in, my friend. It is cocktail time in our world. We need something with more kick than even a good pot of tea. What's your poison? Care for a canapé?"

"Oh, no, no, thank you. I only came to talk to you. And Dr. Kingston, you would be a plus for this."

"Why do you look so stressed? Sure a vodka tonic wouldn't help? No? Then sit down and tell us what is on your mind."

"Do you remember—you must remember—there was a fire next door a long time ago? It completely destroyed the old building." I wanted to get right to the point.

"Yes, there was." She looked baffled. "I did not live here then. My parents were still alive, and I was married to, oh, one of those men. We had our own apartment a few blocks away. But yes, I remember it. Certainly. A big mess in the middle of the night."

"Did you ever wonder how it happened?"

"It was a dreadful old building, an absolute wreck. And fires weren't uncommon in those old places. It was tragic—there were deaths—but, dear, it was no more than an old tinderbox, and no one was surprised."

"And do you remember what was there, then, before the fire?"

Kingston looked wary. He knew. I was sure of it. Louisa looked uncertain, then she said, "It was that nasty witchcraft store, wasn't it, Jeremy? No one missed it, you can be sure of that. Though I might have if I'd known my new neighbors would be even more undesirable, albeit cleaner."

"Now, Louisa, you know they are much better neighbors."

"Not lately." She shot him a hostile glance and drained her glass.

"What makes you interested in that event?" He refilled Louisa's glass from a pitcher and topped off his own with a tiny splash while he waited for my answer.

What should I say? My deepening conviction that there was a web of connections between places and fires and lost souls, if only I could knit it all together? That it was a story with no possible conclusion so far? Merely the complete weirdness of witchcraft in my own Brooklyn?

In the end, I just said, "Still trying to understand how this neighborhood kept changing in the last fifty years." I smiled, giving away nothing. "It's what I do."

"Well, now that you have waked up my old brain, I can tell

you there were rumors at the time. If the fire was set, it's the old *cui bono*, is it not? Who benefits? Some gossip even suggested my family did, that we didn't like them as neighbors. We didn't, but what nerve! If only those fools had seen how that turned out. And when the Witnesses bought it for fire-sale prices—ha ha!—I know some people had those thoughts."

"Come on, Louisa! "

"Oh, all right. Unlikely. But gossip is always imaginative."

"You know," Kingston said, "I believe I have something somewhere. A dedication speech or an interview, when they opened the dorm. If I can find it, would you like a copy? The underlying idea was that by building a place of sacred purpose on ground that was damned by Satanism and death, it was redeeming. Something like that."

"That's crazy. That seems so very…"

"Yes. Early American? Even older? Anyway, I'll look for it. It's a long shot—it's been years—but I'll try."

"Thank you." I was a little stunned. Did anyone in twentieth-century New York actually believe that? Who wasn't as delusional as my Jonathan Doe? How was that possible? "Thank you both for talking to me. I need to head home now."

Louisa rang a tiny bell on the cocktail tray, and Sierra appeared. "Please show Dr. Donato out."

"Oh, wait. One last question." I turned to Kingston. "Do you have any idea who said, or wrote, that piece?"

"I do believe it was Daniel Towns. Even then he was involved in their property division."

I stopped myself just in time. I was astonished again. My head was spinning, but not so much I could not take advantage of a private minute with Sierra.

"I'm still trying to find out how to contact Willow Lief. I've met her, but now she has disappeared again. I have her cell phone but she is not answering. You need to tell me, and the police, where she lives!"

Sierra flinched.

"What if she's in trouble? It might not be that she doesn't want to be found." My trump card, though I didn't actually believe it.

"You don't want to know." Sierra whispered it. "It's awful. You don't want to go there."

"Give."

She finally whispered an address. I knew it roughly. It was a world away, a scary part of one of the scariest parts of Brooklyn. She had a point about not going there.

Torres had returned my call while I was at Louisa's. Now there was a text. "At precinct. Come see me if you can. Something for you." I sent back "On way." And then I contacted Chris and Joe and apologized. This day would never end. I briefly wished I had simply stayed at the museum and stuck to work.

I flagged down a cab to run me over to the precinct; it was not far.

"Sit." Torres passed me a typed report. Though it was only a page, I had to read it twice to take it in.

The handwriting analyst said that the letters, which had looked so similar to me, were definitely not the same hand. Louisa's were one writer and Towns's and mine were the same, but someone else, almost certainly imitating Louisa's writing.

"What? How is that possible? Why would anyone?"

"Yeah. What I said, too. The more we learn, the less sense it makes. She noticed there were a few similar words to the Towns letters in the ones you brought over, too. No question about being connected. Somehow."

I barely managed to croak out, "Then you'll want to see this." I handed Torres the DVD. "To make it even more confusing."

She played it on her computer, so I saw it yet again. No more highlights for me, but I pointed some out to her. When it ended, she played it again without a word.

"This man is…"

"Severely mentally ill. Delusional, it seems."

"Yeah. 'Crazy' was the word on the tip of my tongue, but delusional is more politically correct, let's say." She shook her head. "I'll have it analyzed by a shrink. This is beyond my pay grade, that's for sure. Except..."

"Yes, that's what I thought. Except." I slid my notes to her, the pages and the two columns where I carefully listed things said next to things from the letters next to Witness writings.

As she scanned them over, she muttered to herself and ticked items off with a pen. "And who'd you say he is? This raving lunatic?"

"Don't know." Before she exploded, I quickly went on, "He was called Jonathan Doe when he was brought in as a patient at Downtown Care. He used to sneak out regularly, and then one time, he got lost, they think, and died on the street."

She looked up sharply. "Recently?"

I nodded, and she swore. "I know him now. A rambler. The first real break, and we can't even ask questions." She swore some more, fluently. I was kind of impressed.

I told the rest of the story, how I'd found out about him and who gave me the tape and all the tidbits I had picked up along the way.

She stood up suddenly and grabbed her gear. "What am I waiting for? I need to know what this Lief person knows. Not give her another second to disappear." She leaned out her door and called for Kahn. I stood up.

"I need the address." She had her phone out to tap it in.

"I'll tell you in the car."

"What? You're not coming. You'd only get in the way. I'm not expecting trouble, but who knows? Especially around there. Don't be ridiculous."

"I'm coming." I returned her hard look stare for stare. I hadn't known I had it in me.

She swore again. "You got me. If I thought we were arresting anyone, not a chance—you'd give me that info like it or not—but this is only asking questions. A whole lot of them."

It was an old and shabby apartment building, much worse than Leary's, built from the start to be neglected. It was in the dark under the elevated train tracks. I thought it must be one of the few areas left in Brooklyn with not a trace of gentrification. We came to a stop at a door with a broken lock, squeezed between two shabby storefronts. Even in plain clothes, my companions were recognized as cops, and the few people on the street promptly drifted off.

We went into a foyer, which was reeking and filthy, with no working lights, and went up to the third floor. I was afraid to touch anything, and heard skittering on the floor, too. I was trying to remember why I had insisted on coming. I could not think of a single good reason. I hoped I would not embarrass myself by throwing up.

It didn't help that my companions had guns visible, prepared for whatever. Nothing good.

The door of the apartment gave with a slight push. No working locks here.

It was a single room with some kitchen appliances built into one corner and a futon in another corner. A few other pieces of furniture, frames barely holding together, fabric stained with mold and who knows what else.

Doors to the bathroom and the one closet were open, but Torres and Kahn approached them carefully. Was anyone hiding behind the doors? Nope. They were as empty as they seemed.

The bathroom held only dust and a wastebasket. No toothbrush, no medicines, no glass. The closet held only a few wire hangers.

The rusty cabinets over the sink and stove were empty except for a box of health food cereal and a few almost empty jars of natural peanut butter and jelly. The tiny refrigerator held a puddle of melting ice and a container of spoiling organic milk.

Torres and Kahn relaxed their ready-for-anything stance. There was nothing to be ready for.

"She's gone. Damn!" She turned to me. "What the hell? Did you say anything to her? Did you tell her we would come?"

"No. No. We just talked. No reason for her to run." Was there?

A manila envelope stood up on a cushion of the rotten-looking sofa. No name, only a large drawing in purple marker, a complex three-pointed knot. I knew it. I knew I had seen it before. I closed my eyes and thought. On the cover of books. And on a chain around Willow's neck under her raggedy clothes. And on Sierra's arm. It was a Wiccan symbol, a form of a Celtic knot, a symbol of female power. I thought it was.

While I was thinking, Torres was carefully opening the envelope. A small pistol fell out and a piece of paper.

This time it was Kahn who swore, surprised, and Torres, who was breathing hard as she carefully opened the folded paper. I read over her shoulder.

In tiny, elegant script, spiky, almost runelike, it said: "Not much more left to my life this time around, so I leave you an answer. Did you work out the riddle of Jonathan Doe's life? Haunted by a terrible thing he did. His demons were real. He saw them and they commanded him. But his friend—his friend!—his very best friend!—advised that the best help is the compassionate god who is always near the broken soul. Wrong, wrong, wrong. So then the Goddess told me how to finish this. The circle is closed at last."

"What the hell? Give me an ordinary drugged-up gangbanger. She saying what I think she is?"

"I don't know. I don't know! But we can find out. Looks like the right type of weapon. There's nothing else here. Take some pictures, and get it all back. And you—" She turned to me. "We're going to ask you questions and make a record of it. Everything you know."

"I've told you all of it."

"Not good enough. I want a record, beginning to end."

By the time I walked out, it was dark. I could barely speak. I could barely even think. Too damn much had happened in this one crazy day, and all I wanted was to be home, head on Joe's shoulder, eyes closed, brain switched off.

Joe was happy to oblige, but Chris had teenage things that needed a mom's attention. I had to tell myself to be glad that she still did need me, but at that moment I could barely process my own day, let alone hers.

I finally said, "Do you have any bubble bath?"

She stopped in mid-story. "Uh, yeah? Lemon? Got it for my birthday." She really looked at me for the first time that evening. "Did you have a rough day?"

I nodded. "Leave it in the bathroom, OK? And we can talk more in the morning."

I fell asleep in the tub. I knew because I suddenly couldn't remember when I'd moved the washcloth or added more hot water. Joe found me later, wrapped in a big bath towel, sound asleep on top of our quilt. He told me that when I woke up with a start and thought it was morning. It was three a.m. I'd been dreaming about symbolic knots and lakes of fire.

In the morning, I rushed off to my day at work. It would be boring, compared to what I had been doing. I couldn't wait. Boring, peaceful, ordinary. It sounded pretty good.

I was sidetracked from the start. Nancy was standing across the street from my house, hands in pockets, straight up and alert. There was no doubt she was looking for me, and she did not look happy. I tried to pretend I did not see her and walked briskly in the direction of my work, but that was an exercise in futility. She moved a lot faster than I could and was beside me before I was partway up the block.

"I want to talk to you."

Oh? I thought. Ha-ha. She never wanted to talk to me before. I didn't say it, but I didn't stop walking, either. Then she was standing in front of me instead of next to me, blocking my way. She was bigger than I am, and angrier.

"You are not slipping away today."

I was trapped. No one was out and near us at that moment. No neighbor to greet and then casually walk off with. Joe had left before me, so ESP would not bring him out to the street. And normally withdrawn into near invisibility, today Nancy had anger blazing.

"All right. You've got me. What is it? But make it fast. I am running late already."

"I want you to leave my kids alone." She had locked onto my arm. She had muscles. I would not be able to make her let go. So I made the quick plan to use my weapon of choice instead. Words.

"What the hell are you talking about?"

"I have a job to do, to protect kids who need it. Sierra's not in my group, but she's young and on her own. You keep harassing her, you answer to me."

"Oh, come on. I'm harassing someone? I asked her for information, that's all. No threat. We were right in Louisa's house, for crying out loud, not some dark deserted spot in a park. For all I knew, you were there somewhere working your magic. "

She faltered and I had my arm back.

"That's it?"

"Yes!'

"Maybe I leaped too fast. But you've been stalking her. You have. And she's still a kid. You gotta leave her alone, or you answer to me. She has, all my kids have, enough to carry."

"OK." The idea of me as a scary stalker seemed absurd, but maybe I had been too persistent? But I also didn't appreciate being accosted first thing in the morning on my own block.

"I've said what I came to say. Believe I mean it, though." She turned away, but now it was my turn to grab her. All I got was a handful of her jacket sleeve.

"Hold up. If I leave her alone, you talk to me instead. Answer a few questions. We are on to something important."

She looked wary but agreed to walk a little with me, and talk.

"You said you knew Daniel Towns for a long time, right?"

She sighed. She didn't like this topic, but she muttered a yes.

"How well?"

"Friend of my parents when I was growing up. They were all rising in the organization, I guess you could say. "

Ah. "Was there another friend?" How in the world could I describe Jonathan Doe? I didn't even know his name, let alone what he looked like then. "Tall and thin? And maybe troubled? Confused?"

"Are you crazy? I was a little kid. I didn't pay attention to their friends. Only if they brought me a treat or played with me. Towns was always a friend, so he was around when I was older."

She was right. She would have nothing to tell me about this mysterious, tormented man. Damn. Okay, another way.

"What do they believe, the Witnesses, about mental illness?"

"Where are you getting this from?" She was edging away from me even as she asked.

"Long story. I'll tell you too, I promise, but for now, I just need to know a little more. I'm putting puzzle pieces together."

Her look was mostly hostile, but she said slowly, "Officially they say it's a disease, and getting help is no more shameful than taking medicine for diabetes or the flu."

"And what aren't you saying?" I knew there was something more.

"There's social pressure? Lots of other worlds have the same. Like, your faith should be enough for any troubles. Like that. And believe me, they don't trust any kind of counselor from outside in case they criticize their idea of the truth. That's truth with a capital T. The one eternal truth. My kids tell me some stories to break your heart."

"Even now, when they say it's an illness like any other?"

"Sure. And it was worse back in the day. They never told us kids, but there were always bits we picked up."

"Kids always know more than anyone thinks."

"You bet. I had an aunt. She used to stay in her house and cry.

And my parents read the Bible to her, and other teachings. And prayed. Oh, they prayed. They said she only needed the Scriptures and the counseling of a mature Christian to help her." She stopped, angry at them or me. Perhaps both. "I haven't thought of this for years and years, and haven't wanted to, either!"

"What happened to her?"

"Don't know. It was when I was still a kid. She went away, they said, to a better place. Hospital? Heaven? They would never let us talk about her after." She stopped again and looked right at me. "Happy now?"

And then she walked away. She had tears in her eyes.

I was sorry. I was. And a little ashamed. But I also thought she'd given me the missing piece. I could tell a story now. I didn't know if it was exactly the true story, but some of it was. I saw it and heard it all the way to work, and when I got there, I closed the door and turned off my phone. I had exactly one hour before I had to meet with someone.

It would be the story of a young man, strictly raised and religious, coming up against a world he did not understand. It included—it especially included—women who were tempting and kind and everything he had been warned against. He was attracted and fearful, and no one in his world understood that he was slowly slipping into illness from which he would not recover.

The Bible verses rattled around in his brain. The ones that said to destroy what did not adhere to the moral code he had been taught. There were other, different teachings, but he had lost the ability to hear them. And so he panicked and did what seemed right as he was commanded. He never recovered from the destruction he wrought, the grief and the guilt.

And a long time later, someone understood who he was and what he had done. She was damaged by his acts but did not blame him. She understood about demons. She did blame the people around him who had not seen the warning signs. Had not responded. Had not helped him.

I honestly did not know, yet, if this was the solution to Towns's murder, but I thought it was a story that made a kind of sense, for the time and place, even though in another way, it made no sense to me.

I began to write it. I had one hour to pull together what I was seeing in my mind and write it down.

Chapter Twenty-One

I was right, though. Eventually, the ballistics report came back to Torres, and she told me. It was the gun that killed Daniel Towns. In her own off-center way, Willow Lief had made a confession.

They still had not solved the poison-pen letters. Of course the ones to Towns had stopped with his death, and that handwriting did match some of the more lucid scribblings Willow had saved. Jonathan Doe had written out his bitterness and there would be no more letters from him to anyone. Neither Louisa nor I received any more of the copycat letters, either. The NYPD no longer cared. I had to accept it. Reluctantly.

Fitz liked the chapter I finally wrote. In fact, he loved it. "Write me two more this good, pronto, and an outline, and I can get you a contract." He actually said that. On the phone. He even mentioned a range for an amount. It was not a lot of money, but it still felt like I'd been struck by lightning. In a good way.

Until then, part of me had thought of every conversation with Fitz as a joke. Even as I tried to do the job assigned, I never really believed it. Now I had to. I managed to say all that to Joe, and my dad, who was there, with so many starts and stops that Dad finally said, "Honey, spit it out or I am going back to raiding your refrigerator."

And then he said, "So when are you going to quit your job and write this book?"

That shocked me all the way into speechlessness, something that doesn't happen very often in my life. And he was not laughing at me for it. Joe was not laughing, either. They looked at each other in a way that made me think they'd already discussed it.

Joe finally said, "You've spent a year in a real grown-up job and I haven't once seen you as excited as the times you were working on this project. How much does that say?"

"No. I need the paycheck. It's security for the first time in my life, ever. Ever! Insurance and retirement. Don't you get it?" My voice was getting louder with each word. "And with Chris going to college? Are you both crazy?"

Before I could stalk out of the room, my dad said, "Aren't you a little old for a hissy fit?"

That made me want to stalk out even more, but something stopped me. Maybe I really was too old.

"So would it help to know that Mom and I started an account for Chris the day after she was born?" He looked tentative and insecure, as if he thought I would be upset with him. I'd never seen that look, and it was not a good one on him. I didn't like it.

"So there's some money for Chris's college. Maybe not the whole shot, but a start."

My eyes began to sting.

By then Joe was next to me on the sofa. "You can go on my health plan as a domestic partner." He grinned. "Let's make it official. "He took my hand. "You've got a chance here, handed to you. Won't you hate yourself if you don't take the leap?"

"But what if I fall?"

"I don't know. No one can ever know that. But you do know you're not alone."

It was all too much. I walked out but not in a huff, explaining that I needed to think, and think hard. I went with Joe's usual advice, exercise, and took a long, chilly walk, all on my own. I might have talked out loud to myself.

And that is how I ended up spending the next month frenziedly winding up my work at the museum while scrambling to rough out another chapter or two. Three days after my last one in the nine-to-five world, I signed a contract with Fitz and began a life in the all-day, all-the-time self-employed world. It was scary. It was exciting. Dad and Joe applauded. Chris claimed she could cope with having me always home, but her expression was apprehensive. It made me laugh a little.

I had stashed that Brooklyn Heights story in a file, to be polished one more time when I sent the others in. Then Joe sent me on one last quest.

He didn't mean to. He asked me, casually, whatever happened with the search for the missing Whitman plaque. He was doing some work in the complex where the original building used to be and ran across some very old plans that mentioned the printing shop.

My only possible answer was "Not a thing." I thought I'd take a breather one afternoon and drop in on Dr. Kingston.

I picked the worst possible day. It was late November, and Brooklyn Heights loses a lot of charm when the biting winter breezes start blowing off the harbor. I could feel the temperature drop with each block I walked toward the water.

I blew into Kingston's lobby and ran right into Mike Prinzig. Not literally this time. He was leaving the elevator while as I was waiting for it. Sharply tailored topcoat, shined shoes, extremely annoyed expression. In my casual puffer jacket and everyday jeans, he never gave me a second glance. Or even a first one. I thought as I rode the elevator that I was not pretty enough today and not impressive enough ever.

Kingston, on the other hand, greeted me warmly, took my jacket, and offered very welcome hot coffee.

"How have you been? It's been a while. And how is Louisa? I have been so busy, I haven't even had a chance to call her."

"Ornery as ever. She's still battling the property issue, so I believe it will go to civil court eventually. Silly contentious woman."

"It seems to me that's what keeps her going."

He laughed a little. "Absolutely right. A good conflict works better than a whole shelf of vitamins. But not all battles are worth the cost. And you? Busy with what?"

I filled him in on my crazy life at the moment—I had not yet left the museum—and explained a little about loose ends.

"And that's what brings me here." I showed him the document Joe had copied for me. "Someone found this, and it reminded me. Did you ever get any further with that missing plaque search?"

"Sadly no. We don't like loose ends, do we? But..."

His phone rang. He glanced at it and made a face. "I have to take this. Please excuse me for a moment. "

I went out to the cramped waiting room to give him some privacy. He closed the door behind me with a sharp crack, but his voice did come through the door. It sounded very intense.

I made an effort to focus on the quite interesting photos on the wall I remembered from the first time I was here.

Now that I knew Dr. Kingston, I was especially interested in the little section of his own work. They were the painstaking depictions of Brooklyn landmarks, with tiny colored blocks of text creating the picture instead of lines. I had to stand with my nose practically against the glass to see it all.

There was a name for it, I was sure, but I did not know it. I knew the words though. Whitman poems, arranged to make a picture of the bridge. A Marianne Moore poem about the Dodgers, showing long-vanished Ebbets Field. A poem by Langston Hughes about a day at the beach, depicting Coney Island.

Art that was charming to say the least, and quite a puzzle to grab and hold the viewer's attention. How steady and skillful his hands must be to create this. Was it colored ink? Or some kind of watercolor? What did I know about art? Nothing. But for two more weeks I still worked at an art museum. I surreptitiously took photos of them with my phone. I would ask someone to tell me more.

And then I looked again and wondered if I could blow up the photos, because I also wanted to bring them over to Sergeant Torres. It was a crazy idea, what I almost thought I was seeing, but maybe not.

Kingston's voice shouted, "No. No! It isn't working. It didn't move her at all, and I am done. It's too risky." There was a pause and then a shouted obscenity about someone's money. I heard a small crash, like a receiver on an old phone being slammed down. He had an old-fashioned phone on the desk.

I hastily went back to looking at the historical photos. I didn't want him to find me peering at his work when he returned.

He didn't open the door for a few minutes. When he did, he smiled at me, apologized for the wait in his normal voice, had normal color in his face, dismissed anything I might have heard with a clipped, "Family matter." But the back of his neck was a fading red, and he kept dropping the papers in his hands. He was more upset than he was admitting.

I wanted to say something nice. Really, I did. But at that moment I wondered how much I knew him. If I knew him at all. Or was I being spooked by my own imagination?

So I babbled polite things about no stress like family stress and apologized for showing up on a bad day.

He protested, said he was always happy to see me, but there was—alas!—no progress on the missing Whitman plaque. We needed to accept that it was gone for good.

He looked far too shaken about something that was only a missing artifact, only an oddity, after all. Did he even have a family to trouble him today? He'd never mentioned any at all.

Not knowing what to say, I boldly changed the subject and told him how much I admired his puzzle drawings. He smiled but not really. It didn't move beyond the muscles around his mouth.

"Oh, yes, micrography. Or typographic illustration is another name. It's a pleasant distraction. Very challenging. It's too hard on my aging eyes now, sadly. It's like a puzzle. I learned to do it after taking a class in medieval manuscripts. Somewhere here I have a copy of a six-hundred-year-old picture of a dachshund all in Hebrew script."

A flood of trivial knowledge. A distraction? And he was not looking at me. He could not meet my eyes.

"That plaque. Some mysteries can't be solved." I was babbling, myself. "Speaking of clichés, did you know they never solved the question of Louisa's poison-pen letters? And mine? And I believe they will stop trying to now. The letters have stopped coming."

He nodded a few times. "I suppose that's a relief for Louisa. Though it didn't seem to change her mind, did it? Or even scare her." Honestly, he sounded like he didn't care at all, but the words were so close to what I had heard him shouting.

The outer door slammed open, and Mike Prinzig stormed in. He didn't even see me in the corner behind the door, so I had a front-row seat to the scene. I made myself as silent and invisible as I could.

"You little academic worm. People don't say no to me. They don't quit on me without finishing the job!"

He grabbed Kingston by his shoulders and shook him as he spoke. Kingston, a heavy man but not as tall as Prinzig, turned white. He muttered, "Get out of my office," but he couldn't muster up any authority for it.

As quietly as I could, I dug around in my bag for my phone.

Prinzig stepped back, breathing hard, his face red. "You owe me. If the letters didn't work, come up with another plan. Now. Today. I'm fed up with this."

Kingston gripped the doorframe for support, took a huge, gasping breath, and muttered, "No. I said we're done. I never should have…"

"Yeah, but you did. You have a nice sum of money from me,

you underpaid peasant, and promised you could do it, scare her into leaving. Dumb idea from the start!"

Kingston looked right at him for the first time. "You came to me. It was your idea."

"Like hell it was. I have ideas that work. Except that I counted on you. That was my only dumb move."

My fingers connected with my phone, and in the process I managed to loudly spill the contents of my purse. Prinzig turned and shouted, "Who the hell are you? Who the hell is she, Jer? Why is she here, listening?"

"She doesn't matter." He shot me a pleading look. Was he saying be quiet? "She was here for a meeting. She doesn't know anything about this. She should go, right now."

Prinzig looked at me with intense, narrowed eyes. "Do I know you? "

"No. No way you'd ever have run across her. Let's boot her out of here while we finish our business."

"Wait one minute. I *have* seen you before. We didn't have a wild night. You're not my type. And not in business." He stared at my baggy mom jeans and Gap sweater. "You don't look like any businesswoman I'd be dealing with." He seemed to be ticking categories off in his head. "Definitely not one of my wife's friends. They have style and class."

I was keeping quiet, trying to shrink into the wall, willing myself to be as anonymous as my casual clothes.

"Hey, Kingston, isn't she the girl who asks questions?" He didn't wait for an answer. He knew. He stared at Kingston, then back at me. "Oh, yes. You've been around me, listening and watching. Little spy, right?" He really had me pinned with his fierce expression, and he stood close, too close for me to make a break. Or even breathe. Without moving his gaze from me, he barked to Kingston, "In cahoots? You and her? Did you have blackmail in mind?"

"No! Don't even think it. She dropped in to..."

Suddenly Prinzig stepped back, straightened the lapels of his elegant coat, shot his cuffs, smoothed his hair. He smiled with a lot of teeth. "It doesn't matter, after all, does it? She didn't learn anything today, and nothing we discussed could make trouble for me. And who'd believe a little nobody like you, anyway? You heard we tried to negotiate with old lady Louisa. It didn't work. End of story."

The smile vanished as he looked from me to Kingston and back. "Recommend you not try to make something of it. Really. I do recommend that. Trust me."

And he was gone, slamming the door behind him. I could breathe. Kingston's normal color returned.

"But we aren't done," I said. He still couldn't look at me. "It was you, wasn't it? The letters." I was sure, but it was hard to get the words out. "Why would you do that? Scare an old woman who was your friend?"

"Friend? Only when it suited her. And they were only letters. Harmless paper."

"Oh, give me a break! You meant her harm. You teamed up with people who meant her harm. What were you thinking, working for him? I can hardly even imagine the two of you in the same room, let alone in the same conversation."

He finally looked up at me with a faint trace of an expression. "Believe me, it wasn't easy."

"Then why? Why did you do it? Something so malicious and so childish, even? Did you enjoy it?" Were you the same as any bully I had met over the years? I thought but did not say. Not yet.

He collapsed onto a chair and was breathing hard before he answered. "Enjoy it? No, no, no, not even a little! It was—it started as a joke. *His* joke. He knew about Towns getting letters, and he was talking to me about how to convince Louisa to give up and give in. And he said if only she could be scared off like that, and did I know a way? And I did. Make it look like the same threats. And *he* said, can we find someone who could imitate the other writing? Honest to God, he was laughing! It started as a joke. A prank."

"A prank? By grown men? You must be kidding." But I knew he wasn't. "And then you told him you could do it? You have the skills. You could do the writing? Was that when he stopped laughing?"

He couldn't look up, but he nodded.

I dropped into the other chair so I would be face to face with him. "Come on, Dr. Kingston! This isn't you, is it? How did you come to be talking to him in the first place?"

"At a party." I could barely hear him. "He cornered me. Insisted I talk to Louisa, warn her to be reasonable."

"'Reasonable' meaning to do what he wants?"

"What else? To sell him her whole property, that's what he really aimed for."

"Fat chance."

"Yes. I tried to tell him, but he doesn't hear 'no.' Just not in his vocabulary. And he's—for a dumb guy, he's smart. Sees right into your mind and knows how to use what he finds. Everyone has something. He tried to find hers, her weak point." His voice sank so low I had to move my face in close to his to hear him at all.

I almost reached out to hold his hand. Almost. But I remembered how I felt with his nasty letter in my hand.

"What could possibly be your own weak link? Money?"

"More important. My home. *My* home. My landlady died. Her family was selling the building. Beautiful Victorian building." His voice shook. "I've lived there for decades. Rent stabilized. It was my home, whoever owned it. In *my* neighborhood. How do I move myself and my things, my treasures, at my age? Start all over? And for cheap." He finally looked up at me with a face full of fear. "I'm a retired college professor making a pittance working part-time for the council. Where do I find a place I can afford anywhere in Brooklyn? Anywhere I could live? Bushwick with the baby hipsters? Dear lord." He looked ill. "At my age? And how do I start all over? But Mike Prinzig? He could fix it. Find me a place." He looked down again. "He figured out that's what would get me. And it did."

"And did he? Fix it?"

"Not yet."

He pushed himself up out of his chair and opened the office door. "Time for you to go. We're done. I'm done."

I was relieved. I couldn't wait to get out of there. I went straight to Torres.

I believe he knew I would, because by the next morning, he had already resigned from his position with the council, effective immediately, and could not be reached at the office phone or by email.

Meanwhile, Torres was not as excited by my story as I expected.

"Yes, it solves a mystery. So what? There's hardly a crime here. I can't arrest two citizens for behaving like sixth graders, now, can I?"

"But."

"Oh, please. I have real crimes to handle here. Ya know? This isn't Mayberry RFD."

Then she took pity on me and added, "Look, the DA's office will laugh in my face about this. Yes, I'll look into it. Do you want to follow it up? Press charges, if asked?"

I know I hesitated.

"Yeah. Like I thought. I'll talk to Mrs. Gibbs, too. Or send someone. Or wait and see what the DA office says. You've heard the intro to *Law and Order*? The part about two separate yet equally important groups? This would be theirs."

"The district attorneys who prosecute the offenders?"

"Yeah, them. Their call." She smiled. "Don't look so sad. You have the end of your story, right? Now go on. I have to investigate a real crime or three."

I hate loose ends. I always have, but what she said was true. Fitz loved the revision to my chapter, and there was nothing else on the letters. No further reaction. Louisa was shocked deeply by the story and said it would make her too sad to pursue any action against Dr. Kingston. She would be too busy fighting with the Prince organization about her property. And if she could find a way to use my research in that ongoing battle, she would be happy to do that.

But she did ask me to talk to Jeremy Kingston if I could. Find out if he was all right, even though he'd been a false friend. She had his address. And I had some things for her, too. It was neat stack of mail, the items that had been stuck haphazardly in one of the albums.

Her face brightened at the magazine. "I wondered where that had gotten to." Then she looked over the loose letters and turned pink. She sat down suddenly.

"So you know, now?"

Her voice shook.

"Well, I can make a good guess." I said it as gently as possible. There was a letter from a doctor, a list of appointments, some financial papers, all from a famous cancer hospital. "That's where you were, those times you wouldn't tell anyone?"

She nodded once. She could not, or would not, look at me.

"It's my private life," she muttered. "I am not obligated to share it with the NYPD or the news media or anyone."

"Or friends?"

"Them least of all. I don't want pity, and I don't want help, either. People hovering around, asking how I am? Never, never, never." She finally turned to me. "You know Dylan Thomas? I'm with him, not going gentle into the dark night. Hell, no." She sank into thought and then surprised me. "I did know him, you know, Dylan Thomas. Met him in a Greenwich Village bar one time. He was a drunk, but he was right about this. You will keep this to yourself." It was not a question.

"I think you're wrong not to tell the people who care about you." It was hard to say.

"You, my dear, are a whippersnapper." She almost smiled. "You do not get to have an opinion. Promise?"

"I will keep it to myself." I would, too, but that didn't mean I would not try to change her mind.

Before I left, Kingston's address in my pocket, I did the unthinkable. I hugged her. I don't think I imagined she hugged me back.

I found Kingston in a charming apartment with a fireplace in a Victorian apartment building, probably one of the first in the neighborhood. There was even a turret at one corner that formed a nook in his living room. No wonder he did not want to leave.

It was stripped almost bare and full of cartons.

"I have to be out in two more days. Why are you here?"

"Louisa sent me."

"Ha. She wanted you to yell at me? Beat me up?"

"No. She is way worried about you."

He stopped his rummaging through the boxes.

"Now? Now she is worried, after it is too late?"

I stared at him, and he stopped. "I don't—I wouldn't—I really don't deserve her concern. I know that."

"I agree. But she asked me to find out."

"Well, tell her I am not getting away with my bad behavior." He smiled the least convincing smile I have ever seen. "I am moving to Mesquite, Nevada. They play golf there, I am told. And have ballroom dancing. It's eighty miles from Las Vegas, in case you want to know."

I could not find any words for this news. I could not imagine Jeremy Kingston away from New York.

"My only sibling, my sister, lives there, in a house with room. She's been begging me to move in for years, ever since her husband died. Hot as purgatory there, suitably enough. It will be purgatory in every other way for me, too. Not far from where I grew up, so it's not like I don't know what I'm getting into."

"Good grief. How long have you been a New Yorker?"

"Since I was eighteen. Couldn't wait to leave Nevada. You know that line from *Chorus Line* about how committing suicide in Buffalo was redundant? That was me then. So when you think of me, remember that. Me, back home. A life sentence." He got busy with the boxes again and muttered, "I don't even like my sister that much."

Chapter Twenty-Two

Afterwards, the Prinzigs and the Witnesses left Louisa entirely alone. The possible scandal apparently intimidated all of them, an accidental good result. Of course Joe never had any business from the Prinzigs again.

Willow Lief was never found. Whenever I talked to Sergeant Torres she always added, "Yet. We haven't found her *yet*." But I wonder.

We did find Jonathan Doe, though. Or he found us. It was after my book was published.

Yes, I wrote it, and yes, it was published. With Brooklyn always in the news, there was even some buzz. It was very exciting for a very short time, and we even made a little money. Fitz wants to hear my new ideas for the next one. I'm trying to think of some. I was surprised to learn that I loved working for myself. Much as I hated to admit it, Joe and my dad were right. I wasn't meant for a nine-to-five job, after all. And then the book brought me another opportunity.

It seems there are people in Brooklyn who want to know all about their old houses, and would pay for someone to find out for them. We'll see how that develops.

And someone in Ohio wrote a letter to the publisher the

old-fashioned way, on flowery notepaper in an envelope with a stamp. It traveled from mail room to Public Relations and eventually to Fitz, who eventually sent it to me.

She said that the Jonathan Doe I wrote about might possibly, maybe, be a relative. Her mother had been raised in Brooklyn, in the Bethel community, though the family was no longer associated with the Witnesses. In her frail old age, with time running out, she had been talking a lot about the lost little brother, the sweet young man whose behavior had become increasingly troubled, and then bizarre, and who then disappeared altogether. She hoped she might find something that would ease her mother's mind. She included a phone number, so I called.

She was dismayed to realize that he was buried on Hart Island, New York's vast potter's field, a lonely resting place for the unidentified and indigent dead. Their records would have no name for him but the anonymous "John Doe," and there was no way to match my Jonathon Doe to her family history short of exhumation to do DNA sampling. She exclaimed in horror at the very idea.

We talked about genealogists who could do searching on his name for a fee. I told her how to find the Hart Island records, too. And then, just when our initial excitement about connecting had faded away, and we were winding toward saying a disappointed goodbye, she mentioned a photo.

"My mother and him, before he disappeared. There is a Watchtower sign behind them, and tall buildings."

And the light went back on.

"Please, can you send it to me? I'll give you my address."

"I can do better. There is something called scanning. I don't know how to do that, but my grandson does. You could have it tonight."

And there he was, Jonathan Doe, much younger, but it was him. Right there in Brooklyn Heights. And now he had a name. Ben Jackson. And a family. A sister who remembered him with love and believed she would see him soon.

I had something to send her, too, a copy of that old video recording.

Weeks later, I had a letter:

> *I cannot thank you enough. I showed Mom the tape. She doesn't know much these days, but she knew him. She said, "Why, that's Benjamin. Look how old he got." I explained to her that he had passed on, and she cried, but then said, "I know he is at peace now, and he's waiting for me."*
>
> *We are looking into having him reburied here, with other family, and if not possible, we will put up a stone in his memory. The lost lamb is found.*

That was all later, the end of my story, after the book was published. But a lot happened before that.

Joe came home one day and said "We are taking a vacation." He laughed at my surprise. "Don't look so shocked. When was your last vacation?" When I couldn't even come up with an answer, he said, "That's my point," and poured out a packet of brochures and airline information. Flights to Nantucket.

"I thought this would appeal to you. Only an hour by plane. Overflowing with history, cute old inns and houses, bikes, beaches. Maybe see a whale."

"But I'm too busy. I'm editing the book And Chris."

"Your dad will come stay with Chris. She's fine with it. And you can take work if you must. Honest, your laptop will work there."

It did, but I mostly ignored it for one whole, lovely week. We stayed at a prewar inn—the Revolutionary War—with sloping floors, staircases that didn't make sense, a sitting room with ancient books, scones in the afternoon, and a fireplace in the cool evening. Fabulous breakfasts and a picture-perfect garden. Joe enjoyed trying to puzzle out the history of the very old building, and I enjoyed, well, everything. Charming streets and a whole day at the superb history museum and sunsets on the beach, margarita in hand. Maria Mitchell's home and the fantastic sand dunes. The men in red pants and women in hot pink sundresses with matching sandals came to seem another form of local color.

Soon after we made our reservations, Joe had interrupted my reading one night. "I have something special for you to wear on our trip."

I thought it would be a glamorous set of underwear to replace my ancient mom gear. I was hoping for lace and silk, in purple or fuchsia. I looked up ready to be excited about whatever it was.

His expression was odd. There was no shopping bag. He opened his clenched hand to show me a tiny velvet box. There was a ring in it.

"How about Nantucket for a honeymoon?'

What could I say but yes?

Can you plan a wedding in only a few weeks? Yes. Yes, you can. My socially savvy friend Darcy took over as wedding planner and called in a few favors to get us a wedding in the park. I still don't know how she provided the perfect weather. Chris, my only attendant, dragged me into a marathon of online dress shopping, and found me the perfect one. She invited Jared. Louisa Gibbs came, escorted by Leary. Fitz came with a silver pitcher as a gift, and a reminder that the revised book was still due soon.

And Nantucket made the perfect honeymoon.

Much later, after I was working on the next book, and was completely accustomed to wearing a wedding ring again, and Chris was applying to college, a colleague from the Brooklyn Museum called me. Did she remember it correctly, that I had been working with the Museum's architectural sculpture collection? Yes. Oh, good. She was forwarding a letter that they hoped would make sense to me.

It was a note scrawled on notebook paper, not businesslike, not even grammatical, barely legible.

"I head a wrecking crew team. Takin' apart an old building, in the basement, guy says to me, 'Hey, boss, this looks like something that ain't junk.' I agree. Any idea what it is? PS We are fans of that show *American Pickers,* so we keep our eyes open for junk that ain't junk. Thanx."

I looked at the bad photo and gasped. Then I got right on the phone to my museum contact and told her not to let this get away. I sent her all the research I had done. It was time for the Walt Whitman plaque to come home to Brooklyn.

AFTERWORD

Since all of my books combine history with fiction, I like to include an explanation of which is which.

The characters in *Brooklyn Legacies* are entirely fictional but the setting is a real and well known neighborhood. Most of what I have written about its history and politics is as factual as I could make it. The Jehovah's Witnesses (the Watchtower Society) world headquarters was located there until recently, including the tunnels and the building with the Watchtower sign on its roof. Robert Moses was, of course, a real person. Truman Capote did live there and wrote about it.

Nancy Long's support group is entirely made up, but loosely inspired by other groups of young people from other strict societies.

There was a witchcraft store there in the 1970s, and I have wanted to write about it for many decades, but it was entirely different from the one in *Brooklyn Legacies.*

The lost Walt Whitman plaque is a real bit of history. Since I am writing fiction, I felt free to give it the satisfying ending that does not exist in real life. Yet.

ABOUT THE AUTHOR

Triss Stein is a small-town girl who has spent most of her adult life living and working in New York City. This gives her the useful double vision of a stranger and a resident which she uses to write mysteries about Brooklyn, her ever-fascinating, ever-changing, ever-challenging adopted home. Brooklyn Legacies is the fifth Erica Donato mystery, following *Brooklyn Bones, Brooklyn Graves, Brooklyn Secrets,* and *Brooklyn Wars.* trissstein.com

Photo by Roberto Falck